EARTH AND SPACE

Susan Mayes and Sophy Tahta

CONTENTS

Designed by Sharon Bennet, Kim Blundell, Lindy Dark, Christopher Gillingwater, Steve Page and Mike Pringle

Illustrated by Richard Deverell, Brin Edwards, Chris Lyon, Joseph McEwan, Martin Newton, Mike Pringle, John Scorey, Chris Shields, Guy Smith and Stuart Trotter

WHAT'S THE EARTH MADE OF?

Consultant: Ben Spencer

CONTENTS

Planet Earth

The Earth is a planet which is mostly made of rock. It spins around the Sun in a part of space called the Solar System. There are nine planets in the Solar System altogether.

The Solar System

This picture shows the planets in the Solar System. Each one moves around the Sun on its own invisible path called an orbit.

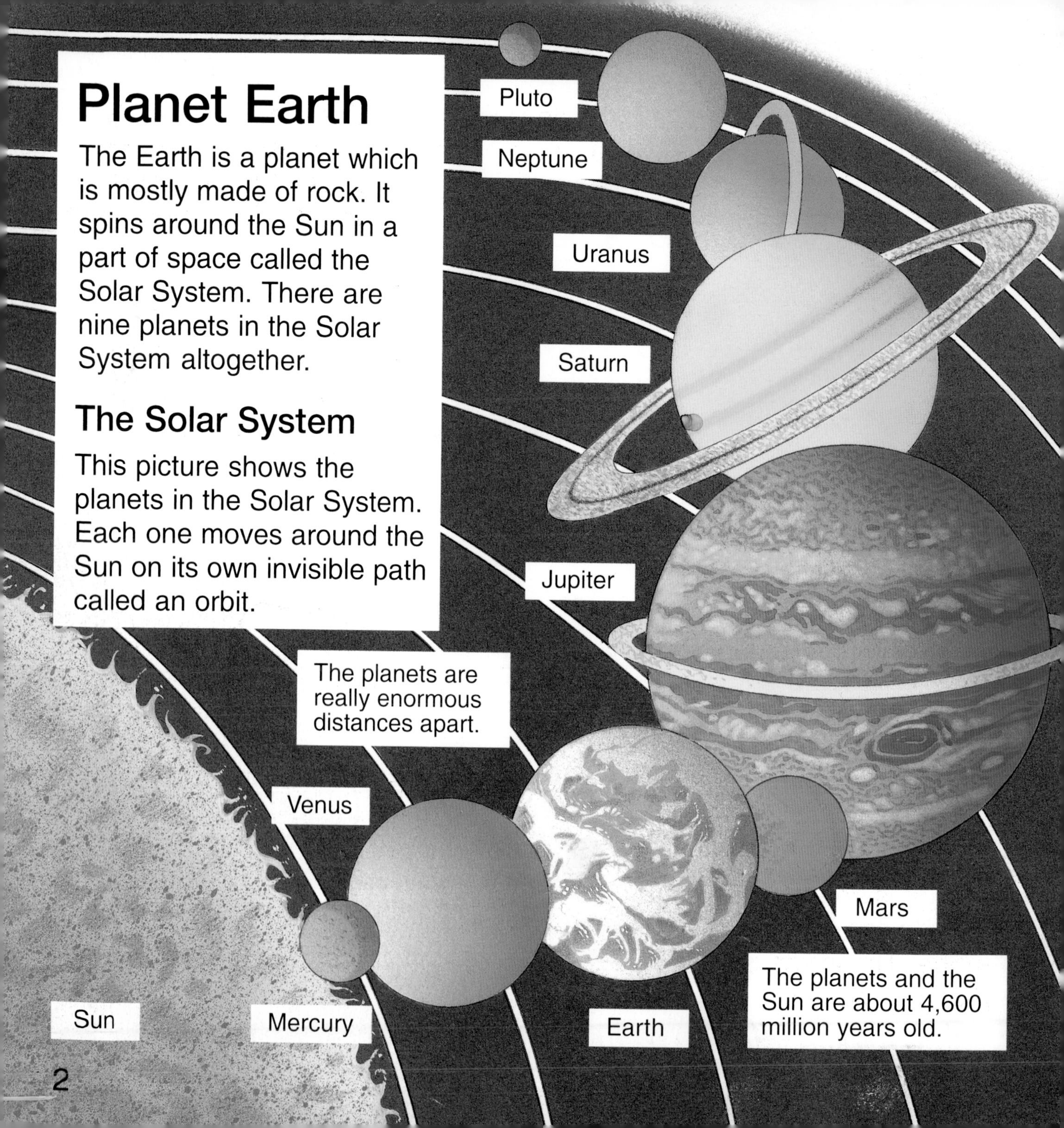

Pluto

Neptune

Uranus

Saturn

Jupiter

The planets are really enormous distances apart.

Venus

Mars

The planets and the Sun are about 4,600 million years old.

Sun

Mercury

Earth

2

The beginning

The Earth probably began as a huge, swirling cloud of dust and gases.

Then the cloud started to shrink. It turned into a spinning ball of hot, runny rock.

The surface cooled and hardened into a rocky crust. Clouds formed and rain fell to make seas.

Inside and outside

The Earth is made up of layers. The thin outer layer is called the crust. It is solid rock. Underneath, there is a very thick, hot layer of rock, called the mantle.

The Earth's middle is called the core. It is hot, runny metal on the outside and solid metal on the inside. The inside is the hottest part of our planet.

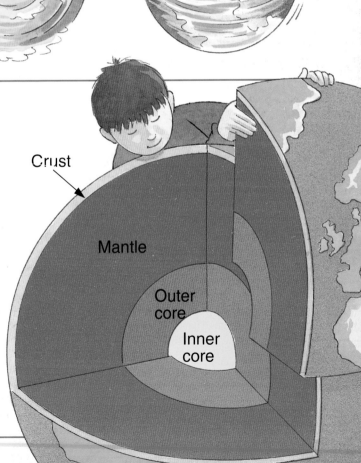

Crust

Mantle

Outer core

Inner core

The big jigsaw

The Earth's crust is not one whole piece, like the skin of an apple. It is made of separate pieces which fit together closely, like a giant jigsaw puzzle. These pieces are called plates.

This flat model shows how the plates fit together.

Sea covers a lot of each plate. Land is the high part of a plate which sticks out of the water.

The edges of the plates are called plate boundaries.

Mantle

How thick is the crust?

The crust is about 5km (3 miles) thick in some places and 70km (43 miles) thick in others. It is very thin compared with what is underneath. If the Earth was the size of a football, the crust would only be as thick as a piece of paper.

Floating plates

The plates float on the mantle. In the mantle there is hot, sticky liquid rock, called magma. The magma churns around and makes the plates move.

4

Before and after

Some scientists think that 200 million years ago, the plates were joined so that the land fitted together as one huge piece. They call it Pangea.

The world today

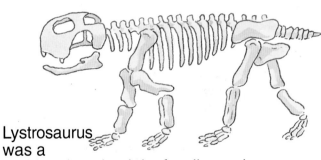

As the plates moved around, Pangea began to split up. The pieces of land drifted apart very slowly and became the shapes we see on maps today.

Pangea

Fossil clues

Fossils are the remains of animals and plants that died long ago. The same sorts have been found far apart. Things probably lived on the same land once, but when it split up, they got separated.

Lystrosaurus was a prehistoric animal. Its fossil remains have been found in countries far apart.

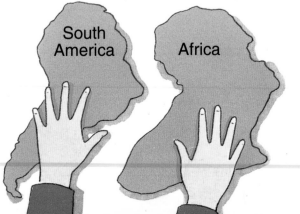

South America

Africa

Fitting together

To see how the Earth's land used to fit together, trace the shapes of South America and Africa from a map of the world and cut them out. Can you tell where the countries used to join?

The changing crust

The Earth's plates move around very slowly. If one plate moves, the ones around it move, too. This makes the crust change in different ways.

Mountains

The world's biggest mountain ranges are made when two plates crash into each other. The crust is pushed up into huge folds, called fold mountains.

Make your own

To make a fold mountain, roll out three rectangles of modeling clay and sandwich them together. Push the ends inward and see how a fold appears.

Layers of folded rock

Folded rock

You can sometimes see rock with folds in it, in cliffs and mountain sides.

Up and down

Plates often move apart under the sea. Magma comes up through the crack. It hardens into a ridge of new crust.

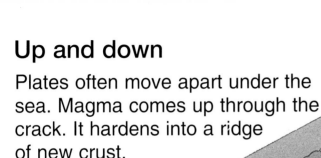

Ridges of new crust

Magma rising

Mantle

This deep ditch is called a trench.

Melting crust

Sometimes, one plate plunges underneath another one. Part of it goes into the hot mantle, where it melts into magma.

Wearing away

Not all of the Earth's surface has been changed by movements in the crust. It has been shaped and worn away by water, wind and ice, too.

Wind throws grit and sand against rocks, wearing them away.

Rock breaks when water freezes in cracks and forces the rock apart.

Thick sheets of ice called glaciers move downhill and grind rock away.

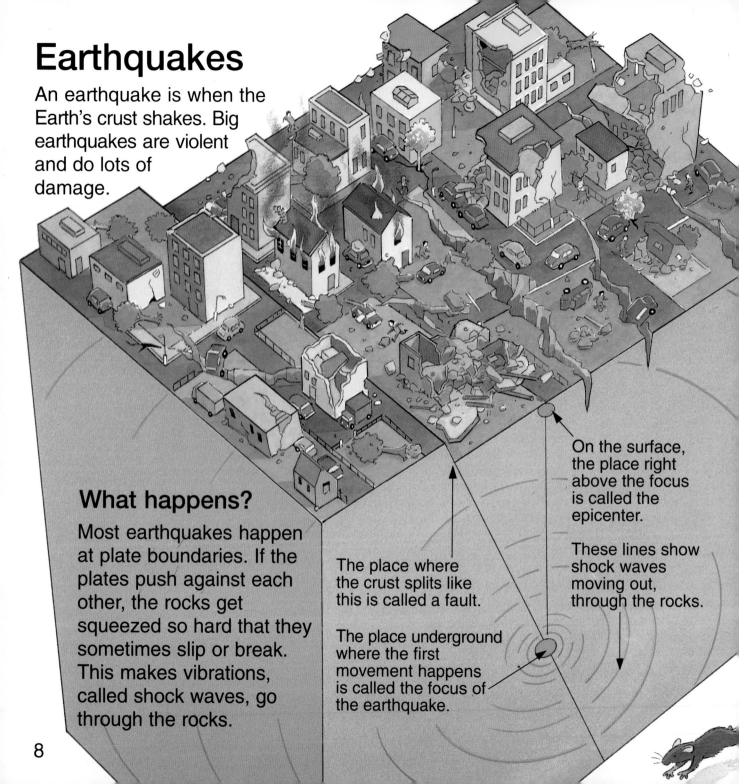

Earthquakes

An earthquake is when the Earth's crust shakes. Big earthquakes are violent and do lots of damage.

What happens?

Most earthquakes happen at plate boundaries. If the plates push against each other, the rocks get squeezed so hard that they sometimes slip or break. This makes vibrations, called shock waves, go through the rocks.

The place where the crust splits like this is called a fault.

The place underground where the first movement happens is called the focus of the earthquake.

On the surface, the place right above the focus is called the epicenter.

These lines show shock waves moving out, through the rocks.

Measuring earthquakes

The Mercalli scale is a list of 12 things which scientists look for, to tell them how strong an earthquake is. As the numbers get higher, the damage gets worse.

At number 3 on the scale, hanging objects swing.

At 8, towers and chimneys collapse.

At number 12, nearly everything is damaged. Big areas of land slip and move.

Animal warnings

Animals have been known to behave strangely before some earthquakes. In China, mice left their holes and ran in all directions.

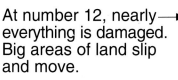

Making shock waves

Machines called seismometers can feel shock waves on the other side of the Earth. Try this experiment to make shock waves for yourself.

Place a piece of paper near the edge of the table and put a little salt in the middle.

Slip one end of a ruler under the paper. Hold the ruler gently as shown in the picture.

Twang the other end of the ruler to make shock waves go along it. See the salt jump.

Volcanoes

Sometimes, red hot magma from the Earth's mantle pushes its way up into weak places in the crust. Then it bursts through to the surface. As it cools, it hardens and forms a volcano. You can see what is going on inside this erupting volcano.

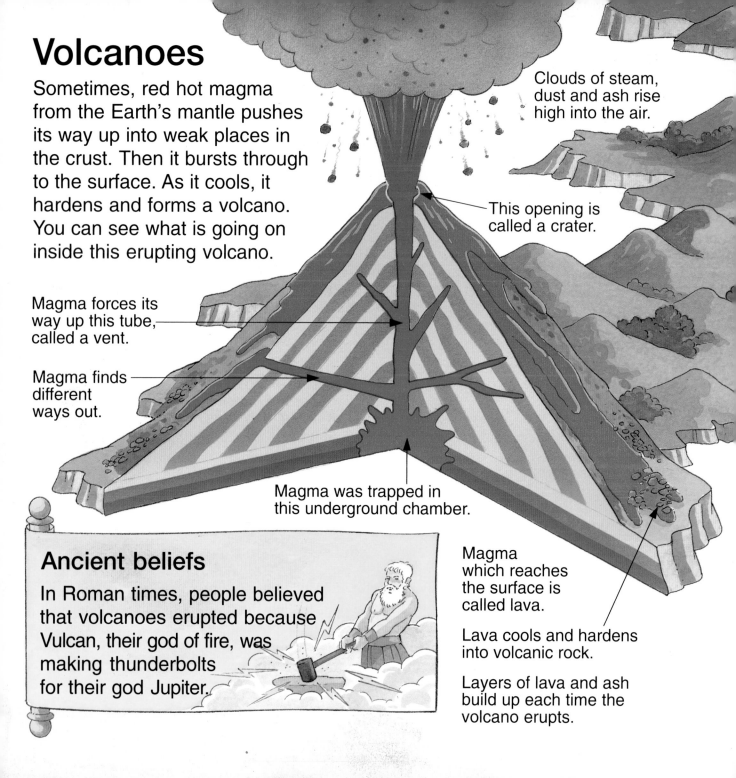

Clouds of steam, dust and ash rise high into the air.

This opening is called a crater.

Magma forces its way up this tube, called a vent.

Magma finds different ways out.

Magma was trapped in this underground chamber.

Magma which reaches the surface is called lava.

Lava cools and hardens into volcanic rock.

Layers of lava and ash build up each time the volcano erupts.

Ancient beliefs

In Roman times, people believed that volcanoes erupted because Vulcan, their god of fire, was making thunderbolts for their god Jupiter.

Different shapes

Many volcanoes are tall cones. This is because their lava is thick and sticky. It does not flow far before it hardens.

Composite volcano

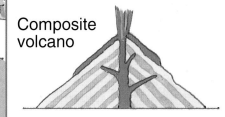

Some volcanoes are fairly flat. This is because their lava is runny. It spreads out quickly before it hardens.

Shield volcano

Volcanic rock

Pumice is a very light volcanic rock. It forms when lava hardens with gas bubbles trapped inside it.

You can buy pumice in health shops, for rubbing away hard skin.

Underwater volcanoes

There are lots of volcanoes under the sea because that is where the Earth's crust is thinnest and weakest of all. Some islands are huge volcanoes which poke out of the water.

Dead or alive?

A live, or active, volcano erupts fairly often. A sleeping, or dormant, one rests for a long time between eruptions. A dead, or extinct, volcano is one which will never erupt again.

Edinburgh Castle in Scotland is built on the remains of an extinct volcano.

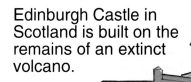

Heat and power

The Earth's crust gives us lots of the heat and power we use in our homes, schools, offices and factories. Here are some of the ways this happens.

Making hot water

In places with volcanoes, the rocks in the crust are very hot. They can make underground water boil and turn into steam.

A geyser is a jet of hot water and steam which shoots out of the ground.

A hot spring is where heated water bubbles up through cracks, to the surface.

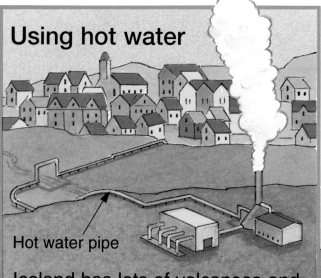

Using hot water

Hot water pipe

Iceland has lots of volcanoes and hot underground water. The water is pumped along pipes to heat many of the buildings there.

Hot rock

Steam power

Some countries make electricity using steam from the Earth's crust.

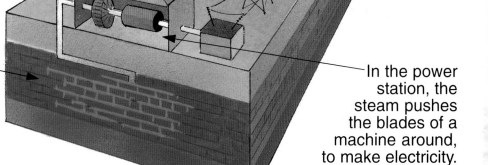

Steam is trapped in this rock.

The steam goes along pipes to a building called a power station.

In the power station, the steam pushes the blades of a machine around, to make electricity.

Underground fuel

Coal, oil and gas are called fossil fuels. They form very slowly in the crust. Coal is the remains of plants that died millions of years ago.

Oil and gas are made from the remains of tiny sea animals and plants. Fossil fuels are used in some power stations to make electricity.

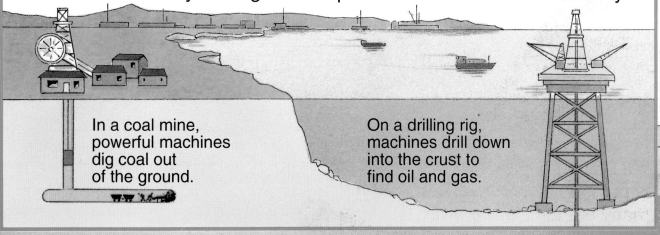

In a coal mine, powerful machines dig coal out of the ground.

On a drilling rig, machines drill down into the crust to find oil and gas.

Igneous rock

The Earth's crust is made up of three main kinds of rocks. Igneous rock is one of them. It is made when magma rises from the mantle, then cools and hardens. "Igneous" means "fiery".

Volcanoes are made from igneous rock. They make more of it each time they erupt.

Sometimes, magma cools and hardens into a huge mass of igneous rock under the ground.

Magma

Granite

Granite is a very hard igneous rock which forms under the ground.

In some places, big lumps of granite stick out of the ground. They were buried once, but the soil and rock above wore away.

Granite is good for building because it is hard and strong.

Sedimentary rock

Earth's rocky crust is being worn away all the time. The tiny, worn fragments help to make new rock called sedimentary rock.

Fragments of rock can get washed into lakes, rivers and the sea. When they settle they are called sediments.

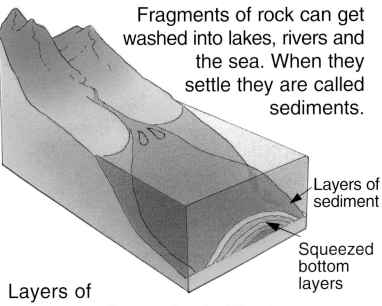

Layers of sediment

Squeezed bottom layers

Layers of sediment pile up slowly. The bottom layers get squeezed together to form sedimentary rock.

Layer upon layer

There are lots of layers of sedimentary rock in the Grand Canyon, in Arizona, USA.

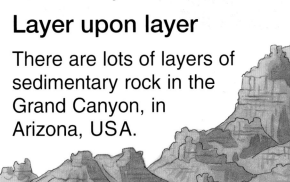

Sandstone

Sandstone is a sedimentary rock made from grains of sand from lakes, beaches or deserts.

You can often see layers in sandstone.

Sandstone is used for building, but it can be worn away by the weather.

New sandstone carving

Old sandstone carving

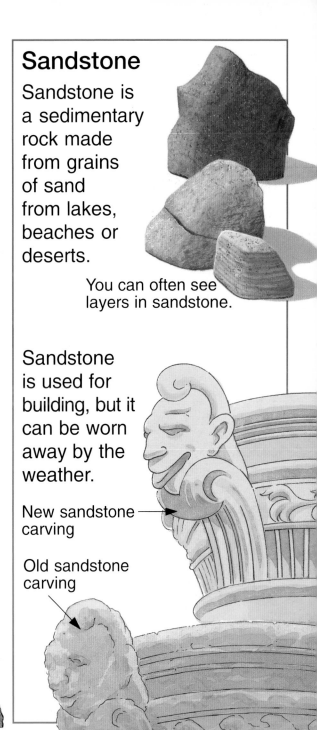

15

Metamorphic rock

Metamorphic rock starts life as igneous rock or sedimentary rock. It is made when these kinds of rocks are squeezed or heated, or both.

When mountains form, all the squeezing and heating make huge amounts of metamorphic rock.

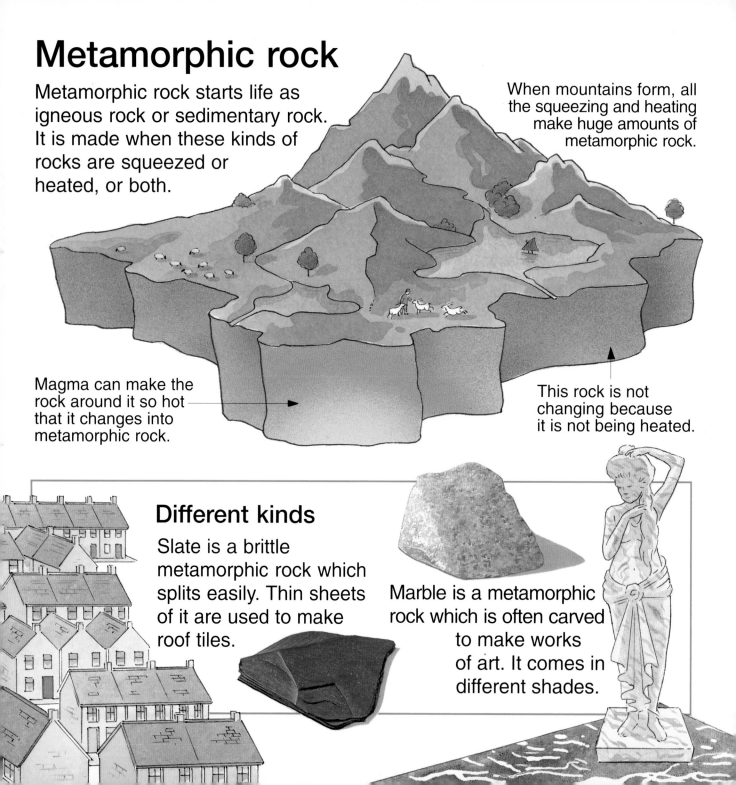

Magma can make the rock around it so hot that it changes into metamorphic rock.

This rock is not changing because it is not being heated.

Different kinds

Slate is a brittle metamorphic rock which splits easily. Thin sheets of it are used to make roof tiles.

Marble is a metamorphic rock which is often carved to make works of art. It comes in different shades.

Rock spotting

You can find different kinds of rocks almost anywhere. Here are some good places to start looking.

Mountains and hills usually have lots of bare rock and loose stones.

Many beaches are covered with pebbles. These are worn pieces of rock.

Buildings, statues and pavements are all made from different kinds of rocks.

Important notes

Never go alone.

Never go near dangerous places such as cliffs and deep water.

Always tell an adult where you are going.

Only collect loose rocks. Never break any off.

Things to take

These things will be useful when you go rock spotting.

A camera for recording things you see in towns.

A notebook and pencil for listing facts about each sample and where you found it.

Small plastic bags for collecting samples.

Felt-tip pens for numbering samples.

A book about rocks to help you find out what your samples are called.

17

Minerals

All rocks are made up of building blocks, called minerals. Minerals come in different shapes, sizes and tints. They form crystals which grow packed closely together.

This is rock seen through a powerful microscope. The shapes are mineral crystals.

Different mixtures

Most rocks are made from a mixture of minerals. Granite is made from three minerals, but it can have different amounts of each one in it. This is why there are different kinds of granite. Here are three of them.

Big crystals

If minerals have plenty of space to grow, they can become beautiful flat-sided crystals.

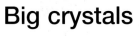
Amethyst

Pyrite

You can sometimes find rocks with crystals growing inside, like this.

Minerals around us

Minerals are taken out of the ground and used to make all kinds of things that we use every day. Can you find any of these things in your home?

Iron ore is a mineral which is used to make cars.

Mirrors are made from minerals called silica and silver.

Quartz is a mineral used in digital watches.

Light bulbs have a mineral called tungsten in them.

Salt is made from a mineral called halite.

Blackboard chalk is made from a mineral called gypsum.

Talcum powder is made from a mineral called talc.

The middle of a pencil is made from a mineral called graphite.

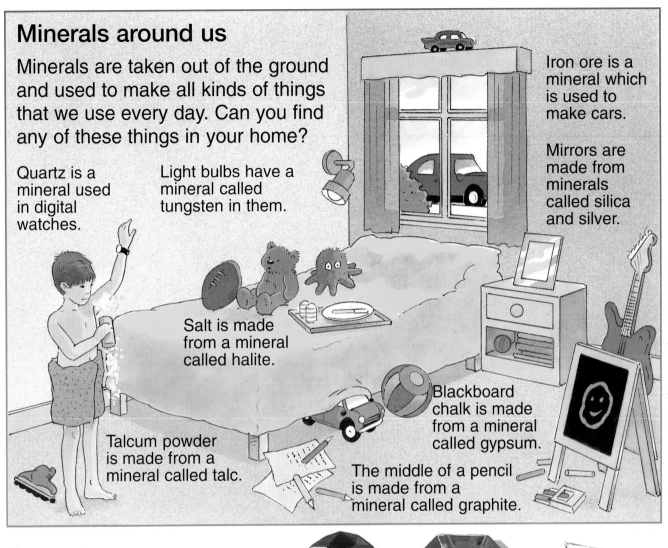

Gemstones

Gemstones are mineral crystals which have been cut into special shapes and polished. They are very hard. They are also beautiful and expensive.

Ruby

Emerald

An uncut ruby.

Diamond

Sapphire

19

Caves

In some places, there are huge caves and tunnels under the ground. They have been carved out by water which has soaked into the soil and rock from the Earth's surface.

Rainwater and water from streams and rivers soak into the ground.

Soaking in

Rock which has tiny spaces or cracks in it lets water trickle through it. Any rock which lets water through is called permeable rock.

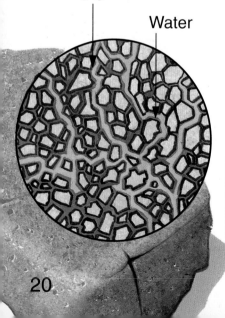

Tiny grains of rock

Water

Sponge test

A bath sponge has spaces in it, rather like permeable rock. Try this experiment to see how water soaks in through the spaces. It works best if you wet the sponge then squeeze it out first.

Put the sponge on a plate and pour water on slowly. Stop when the water starts trickling out.

To see how much water has soaked into the sponge's spaces, squeeze it over an empty jug.

Carving out

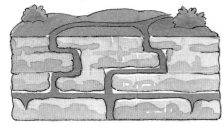

Limestone rock is made up of layers. Cracks between the layers let water trickle through.

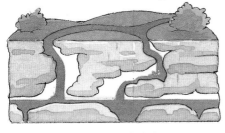

As the water trickles, it eats away at the rock. Very slowly the cracks become tunnels.

When water wears away big areas of rock, a cave is made.

Stalactites and stalagmites

Water drips from a cave roof and leaves behind tiny amounts of minerals. Very slowly, these form rocky icicles called stalactites. Drops hit the floor and towers called stalagmites form.

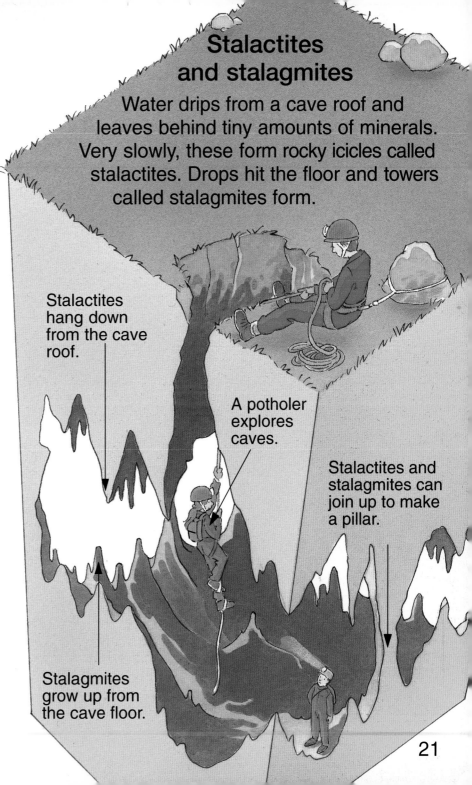

Stalactites hang down from the cave roof.

A potholer explores caves.

Stalactites and stalagmites can join up to make a pillar.

Stalagmites grow up from the cave floor.

21

Fossils

Scientists have found out what lived on Earth millions of years ago by studying fossils. Fossils are mostly found in sedimentary rock.

How fossils form

When an animal dies, its soft parts rot away, but its hard skeleton is left. If it sinks into a muddy place, it gets covered with sediment.

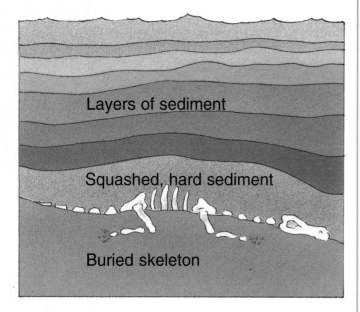

Layers of sediment

Squashed, hard sediment

Buried skeleton

The bottom layers become squashed and harden into rock. Over time, minerals in the rock turn the skeleton to stone. This makes it into a fossil.

Different kinds

There are lots of fossils of sea creatures. This is because sandy sediments covered their dead bodies quickly, before they rotted away or broke up.

This is the fossil of an extinct sea creature called an ammonite. It is about 190 million years old.

Trilobites lived at the bottom of the sea. They are extinct now. This fossil is about 400 million years old.

Shells make good fossils because all of their hard shape turns to stone.

These are fossils of plants called ferns. Ferns like these still grow today.

There are fewer plant fossils than animal fossils. This is because plants have lots of soft parts which do not fossilize easily.

Sometimes, animals' tracks and trails become fossilized. These are called trace fossils.

Dinosaurs often left tracks in soft land. This fossilized dinosaur footprint is about 120 million years old.

Finding fossils

People who study fossils are called paleontologists. Take a close look next time you go to a rocky beach and you may find some fossils yourself.

Fossils are usually found when the rock around them gets worn away.

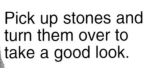

Pick up stones and turn them over to take a good look.

If you want to look at a really good fossil collection, contact your nearest museum to see what they have.

Earth facts

The greatest distance around the Earth is around its middle, called the Equator. It is 40,075km (24,902 miles) around.

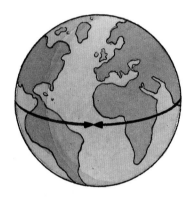

The deepest caves are a group of caves called Réseau Gouffre Jean Bernard, in France. They are 1,602m (5,256ft) deep.

The oldest fragments of the Earth's crust discovered so far are crystals of a mineral called zircon. They are 4,276 million years old.

The highest mountain in the world is Mount Everest, between Tibet and Nepal. It is 8,863m (29,078ft) high.

The highest active volcano in the world is Ojos del Salado, between Chile and Argentina. It is 6,887m (22,595ft) high.

The most expensive gemstone ever was a diamond which someone bought for 12,760 million dollars.

WHAT'S UNDER THE GROUND?

CONTENTS

Under your feet

Under the ground there is a world you hardly ever see. Something is happening down there all the time.

People underground

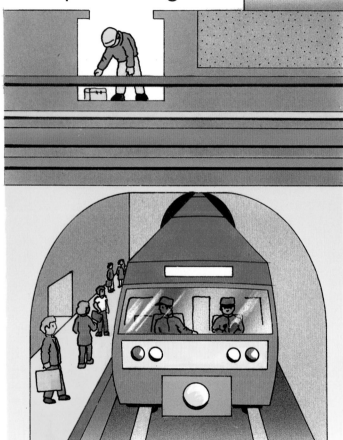

People do different jobs under the ground. They dig and build, or mend things under the street. They even travel through specially made tunnels.

Animals

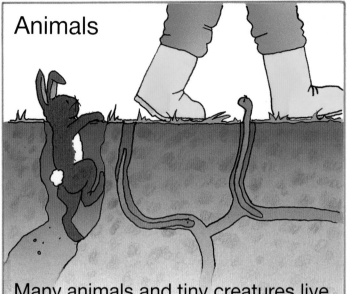

Many animals and tiny creatures live in the soil under your feet. Some of them come out to hunt or play. Others stay underground all the time.

Plants

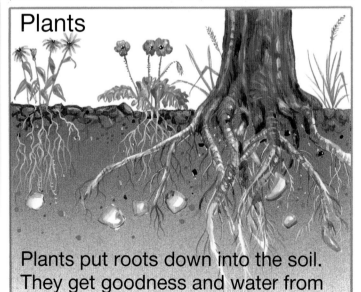

Plants put roots down into the soil. They get goodness and water from it, to help them grow.

Life long ago

The bones of huge creatures have been found under the ground. They were buried for millions of years.

Digging things up

Your home may be made from things which are dug out of the ground. So are lots of things you use every day.

Dinosaur skeletons have been uncovered in some countries. They show us what lived long ago.

There are many things hidden under the ground. You can find out all about them in this part of the book.

Under the street

Pipes, tunnels and cables are put under the street to keep them out of the way. You cannot see them most of the time, but there are clues which tell you they are there.

A metal plate on a wall shows that there is a big underground water pipe nearby.

Under the metal cover is a room called a manhole. Pipes go through it, carrying fresh water.

Rainwater runs through this grate. It goes down pipes which carry it away.

Water pipes

Fresh water for you to drink and use is pumped through the mains pipe.

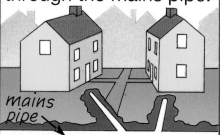

mains pipe

Another pipe joins the mains and takes the water into your home.

Drains and sewers

A drain is a pipe which carries dirty water and waste from your house.

Then the waste runs into bigger pipes. They are called sewers.

Storm drains

Rainwater flows through a grate and fills a pit under the street.

Garbage collects here.

The water runs into a pipe. This takes it to the storm drain.

Most telephone messages travel through underground cables.

When workers dig up the road you can often see electric cables or gas pipes under the ground.

Did you know?

Many telephone cables have thin glass threads inside. Your message goes along one of these.

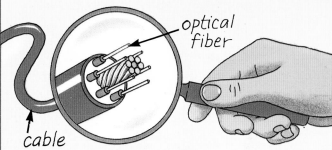

optical fiber

cable

Each thread, called an optical fiber, is as thin as a human hair. It can carry thousands of calls at one time.

Putting electricity underground

Electric cables carry power to homes, schools, factories, hospitals and shops. They often go underground.

First, deep trenches are dug in the street. Pipes called ducts are laid in them and covered with soil.

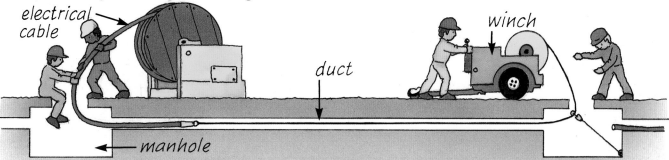

electrical cable

winch

duct

manhole

The electric cable is on a huge reel. One end is put down an electrical manhole and into the duct.

At the next manhole, a winch pulls the cable through. The end will be joined to a cable from another duct.

Tunnels for travel

Many cities in the world have subways. Thousands of people use them every day to get to places quickly and easily.

Building tunnels

The world's first subway was built in London, in 1863.

A huge trench was dug in the road. Railway lines were laid in it and covered with an arched roof. Then the road was built over the top again.

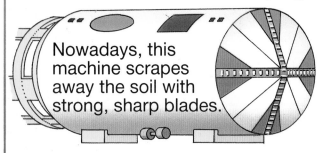

Nowadays, this machine scrapes away the soil with strong, sharp blades.

Today, tunnels are built much deeper under the ground. Machines can drill holes under buildings and rivers.

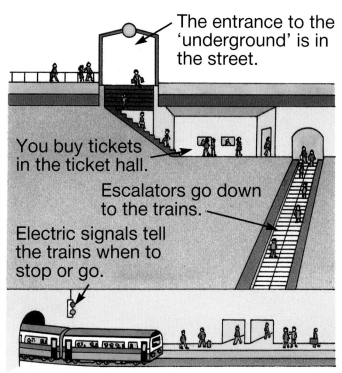

The entrance to the 'underground' is in the street.

You buy tickets in the ticket hall.

Escalators go down to the trains.

Electric signals tell the trains when to stop or go.

Did you know?

In some countries, road tunnels are built inside mountains. The longest one in the world is in Switzerland.

The St. Gotthard Road Tunnel goes through the Swiss Alps. It is just over 16km (10 miles) long.

The Channel Tunnel

The Channel Tunnel is really three tunnels. They go under the sea between Britain and France.

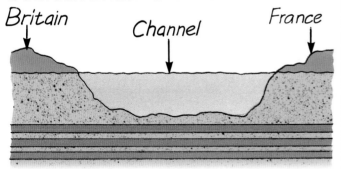

Britain

Channel

France

Now people can travel between the two countries by going under the sea as well as going over it.

Trains carry passengers through two of the tunnels. They can go almost 300km (186 miles) an hour.

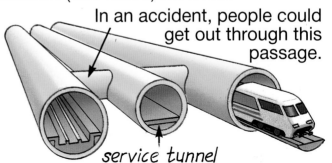

In an accident, people could get out through this passage.

service tunnel

The middle tunnel is called a service tunnel. Workers can go through it when they make repairs.

Lining a tunnel

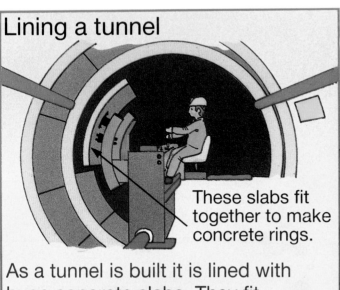

These slabs fit together to make concrete rings.

As a tunnel is built it is lined with huge concrete slabs. They fit together inside the tunnel to make it strong and to keep the damp out.

Electric cables are fixed to the tunnel walls. They work lights and machines.

Tractors and trucks drive around inside the tunnel.

Under your home

Some buildings have rooms underneath. A few homes are built underground. But nearly all buildings begin below the surface.

Building foundations

Builders make the foundations of a house first. These are built into the ground and the house is built on top. They stop the house from sinking.

A digger makes holes called trenches.

The trenches are filled with concrete.

The concrete dries hard to make strong foundations. Walls will be built on top.

Under roads and piers

Roads have strong layers of different sized rocks underneath.

A pier has legs made of iron and concrete. They go down into the sand.

Under a skyscraper

A skyscraper is a very tall building. It is so heavy that it needs special, strong foundations.

The foundations are made by drilling deep holes into the ground. Steel rods and concrete are put into each one.

A city on water
Venice, in Italy, was built over a salty lake called a lagoon.

In Venice, people travel along canals.

Logs were pushed down into the muddy ground under the lagoon. Wood and stones were laid across the logs. The city was built on top.

Basements and cellars
Some buildings have rooms which are lower than the street. This underground part is the basement.

This is a wine cellar underneath a hotel.

A cellar is an underground room used for storing things. Wine is kept in a cellar as it is cool down there.

Underground homes
The Berber people live in Tunisia, Africa. They build underground homes.

The top rooms are used for storing things in.

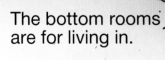

The bottom rooms are for living in.

They find deep pits and burrow into the walls to make rooms. These stay cool in the hot daytime. On cold winter nights the rooms are warm.

Holes and burrows

Many animals tunnel down into the soil to make homes underground.

These homes are safe and hidden away. They have different names.

Badgers live in a home called a set. They rest there in the day and come out at night.

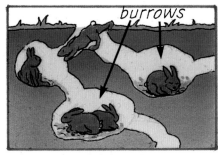

Lots of rabbits live together in a warren. It is made up of groups of burrows.

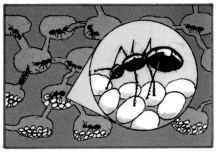

Ants live in an underground home called a nest. It is made of passages and rooms.

Made for digging

Burrowing animals have bodies which are very good at digging.

Rabbits use their front paws to burrow into the ground. They push the soil away with their back legs.

Moles have strong front legs. They can dig easily with their shovel-shaped feet.

Earthworms have strong muscles to pull them through the soil.

Moles live in the dark and are almost blind.

Living in hot places

Deserts are hot, dry places. Most small desert animals live in burrows in the daytime. They come out at night when the air is cooler.

Keeping damp

An Australian desert frog sleeps in its burrow nearly all year.

A special covering of skin keeps it damp. It only comes out when it starts to rain.

The fennec fox hunts at night and rests in its burrow in the day.

The jerboa comes out to search for seeds and dry grass.

Living in cold places

Animals live in some of the coldest places in the world. Many survive by eating a lot, then sleeping all winter. This is called hibernation.

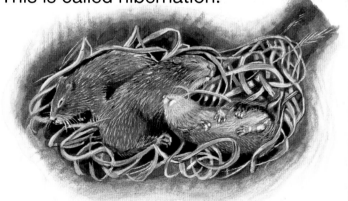

The animal which hibernates the longest is the Barrow ground squirrel. It sleeps for nine months.

Families of marmots hibernate inside their warm burrows. They make grass nests and block the way in.

What's in the soil?

Soil is really layers of stones, sand and clay. These come from rock which has been worn away by water and wind. This takes millions of years.

Nothing would grow without humus. This is made from dead plants and animals which have rotted away. The soil on top is full of humus.

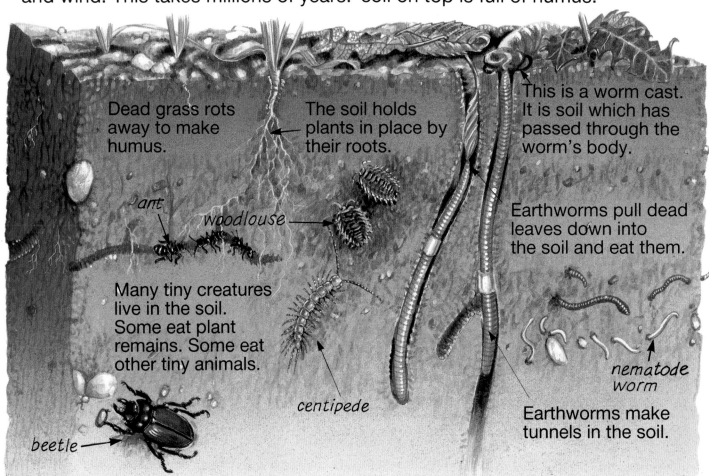

Dead grass rots away to make humus.

The soil holds plants in place by their roots.

This is a worm cast. It is soil which has passed through the worm's body.

ant

woodlouse

Earthworms pull dead leaves down into the soil and eat them.

Many tiny creatures live in the soil. Some eat plant remains. Some eat other tiny animals.

nematode worm

centipede

beetle

Earthworms make tunnels in the soil.

Humus changes into something called minerals. All living things need minerals to help them grow*. Minerals feed plants with goodness to make them strong. Earthworms help mix the minerals into the soil. Plants also need air and water. These get into the soil through tunnels made by worms.

36   *Calcium is a mineral, for example. It makes your teeth and bones strong.*

Making a wormery

Fill a jar with layers of soil and sand. Make sure the soil is damp, then put some leaves on top.

Cover the jar with a cloth.

Put a few worms in the jar, then cover it up so it is dark. The worms will start to tunnel. In a few days the soil and sand will be mixed up.

Wet and dry soil

Sandy soil is dry because water drains through it. Desert plants grow well in this kind of soil.

cactus

sandy soil

They would not grow in soil with lots of clay in it. Clay soil holds water easily. It is wet and sticky.

Food under the ground

Gardeners often grow plants in the same place every year. The minerals which feed the plants get used up.

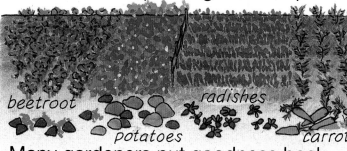

beetroot

radishes

potatoes

carrots

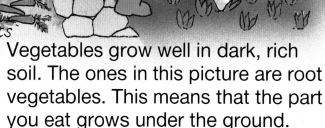

compost heap

Many gardeners put goodness back into the soil by digging in compost. This is made from plants which have been specially left to rot away.

Vegetables grow well in dark, rich soil. The ones in this picture are root vegetables. This means that the part you eat grows under the ground.

About fossils

Fossils are the remains of animals and plants which lived millions of years ago. This picture shows an animal which died and sank to the sea bed. The soft parts of its body rotted away, but the bones were left.

sea

sand

sediment

bones

The bones were covered with sand and tiny grains called sediment. The sediment turned into hard rock and the bones were trapped inside.

Very slowly, minerals in the rock changed the bones into fossils. These stayed buried for millions of years until the rocks were uncovered.

What fossils tell us

The fossils in these pictures helped scientists to guess what the first living things looked like.

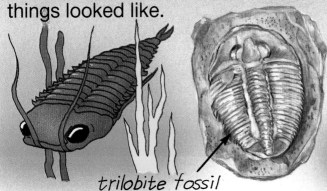

trilobite fossil

stegosaurus fossil

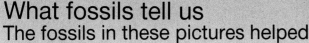

The first animals lived in water. Trilobites were sea creatures with hard bodies made of segments.

Later, dinosaurs ruled the Earth. Stegosaurus was a dinosaur with lots of bony plates along its back.

Plants long ago

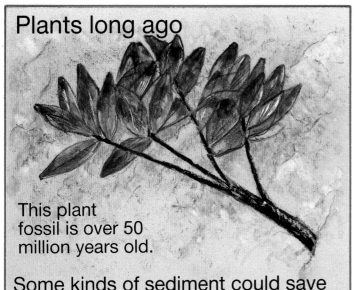

This plant fossil is over 50 million years old.

Some kinds of sediment could save plant shapes for ever. There are many fossil remains of the first plants.

Looking for fossils

Fossil hunters do not usually find anything as huge as a dinosaur. But they do find lots of other fossils.

This special hammer helps to get the fossil out.

Rocky beaches are good places to search. A rock may get worn away and part of a fossil is uncovered.

arsinoitherium fossil

fossil of a footprint

Millions of years later there were animals almost like those we see now. This one was like a rhinoceros.

The first kind of human lived around 2 million years ago. The oldest human fossils are from Africa.

Inside a cave

A cave is like an underground room. It is made by rainwater which wears rock away. Caves often form in limestone which wears away easily.

Water drips from the ceiling. It leaves minerals behind. Very slowly these begin to form rocky icicles called stalactites.

Drops with minerals in may hit the floor. They make rock towers called stalagmites.

An underground stream runs through this cave.

The water trickles down into holes and passages in the rock. It makes them bigger and bigger. A cave is a huge hole which has been made.

What lives in a cave?

Most animals living in the mouth of the cave also live in the outside world. Cave swallows fly in and out.

It is darker further inside. It is also damp and cool. Bats live here and come out to hunt at night.

Deep inside the cave it is dark all the time. Glow-worms may live in here. They make their own bright lights.

A hidden cave

The way into a cave is sometimes hidden. In 1940 two boys discovered a cave which nobody knew about.

The boys were walking their dog near Lascaux in France. They found the cave when the dog fell down the entrance which had bushes in front.

Cave paintings

The Lascaux cave has paintings on the ceiling and walls. Cave people did them thousands of years ago.

The cave people made their own paints and tools. They painted bulls, cows, deer, bison and horses. These were the animals they hunted.

Try this

Do a painting using tools and paints which you have made or found yourself. You will need:

Large scrap of paper or cardboard

water

soil in a pot

twigs

You could also try painting using food coloring in a few drops of water.

Mix a few drops of water into the soil. Cave people used colored earth to make paint. They mostly used red, yellow, brown, black and white.

Dip the twig brush into the paint and try painting on the cardboard with it. You may need to dip it in many times as you work, but keep going.

Useful things underground

People dig and drill for things far underground. Coal and oil help to make electricity, but they are also used to make lots of other things.

Coal

The coal is cut out by this machine.

Coal is made from rotted trees and plants. It began to form millions of years ago. People work in mines to dig coal out of the ground.

Things from coal

paint

plastic

perfume

soap

black lead in a pencil

Coal is treated in a special way so it can be used to make lots of things you use at home. Here are some of them.

Oil

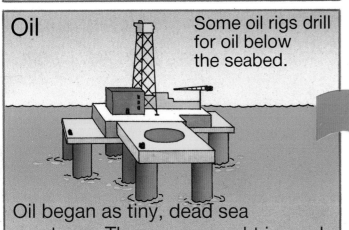

Some oil rigs drill for oil below the seabed.

Oil began as tiny, dead sea creatures. They were caught in mud which became rock. Slowly they turned into oil and gas. On a drilling rig machines drill down for the oil.

Things from oil

dishwashing liquid

gasoline

plastic

dye to color material

If oil is heated to just the right temperature, it can be made into the things you can see above, and more.

Things for building

For thousands of years homes have been built using different kinds of rocks. They are dug out of the ground in places called quarries.

Clay is made from tiny grains of rock. Damp clay is made into shapes and baked hard to make tiles.

Glass is made by melting limestone, sand and something called soda.

Bricks are made from clay.

Building blocks are made of concrete.

Concrete is made from small stones, sand and cement. These are mixed with water and left to harden. This makes a very strong building material.

Metal from the ground

Metal is found in rocks. You can find lots of metal things in your kitchen.

tin cans
cutlery
taps
oven
sink

Rock with metal in it is called ore. Some kinds of ore are heated in a special oven. The metal comes out as liquid ready for making things.

Did you know?

Jewels form deep inside the Earth where it is very hot. Minerals far underground turn into hard crystals.

diamond

Quartz is used in digital watches.

ruby   quartz

These crystals are rough when they are taken out of the ground. They are cut and polished to make jewelry.

43

What's inside the Earth?

The Earth is like a ball with a hard, rocky crust. Some parts of the crust are weak and it often moves or cracks in these places.

Underneath the crust is the mantle. This is hot, soft rock which moves all the time.

crust

mantle

outer core   inner core

The middle of the Earth is called the core. The outside of the core is hot, runny metal. The inside is hard metal. This is the hottest part.

Sometimes the inside of the Earth moves so much that amazing things happen on the surface, where we live.

Volcanoes

A volcano is made when hot, runny rock is pushed up from inside the Earth. It hardens into a cone shape.

This volcano is erupting. Hot rock called lava is bursting out of it.

This lava will cool and harden into a layer of rock. The volcano gets bigger each time it erupts.

crater

Some cone-shaped mountains are old volcanoes. They are extinct. This means they do not erupt any more.

Shaking ground

An earthquake is when the ground shakes very hard. It happens when the Earth's crust moves suddenly.

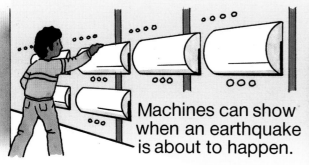

Machines can show when an earthquake is about to happen.

In countries with many earthquakes the buildings must be specially made, so they do not fall down.

Hot water

In some places a fountain of hot water shoots out of the ground. It is called a geyser. The water is heated by hot rocks in the Earth's crust.

This geyser in America spouts water about once an hour.

In some countries they use underground heat to make electricity.

Buried treasure

Vesuvius is a volcano in Naples, Italy. It first erupted nearly two thousand years ago, in Roman times.

These are Roman treasures.

gold earring

gold bracelet

bead and stone necklace

The towns of Pompeii and Herculaneum were buried under ash and mud. They were found again by accident, nearly 300 years ago. Many beautiful treasures were uncovered very slowly and carefully.

Underground facts

On this page you can find out about some amazing things underground.

The longest tunnel

The longest tunnel is almost 169km (105 miles) long. It carries water to New York City, USA.

It is just over 4m (13ft) high. That is about as high as two tall people.

The first bird

A fossil of the first bird that ever lived was dug up in Germany, in 1861. The bird was called Archaeopteryx. It lived over 150 million years ago. You can even see the feathers on the wings and body.

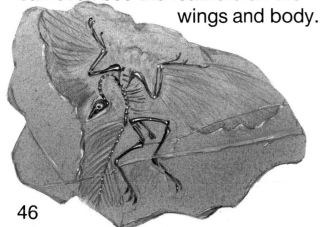

Going down

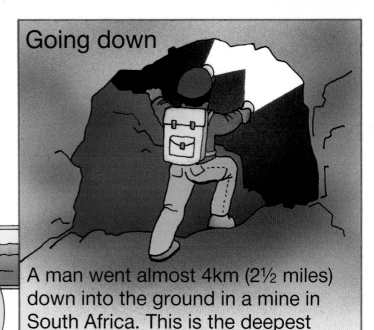

A man went almost 4km (2½ miles) down into the ground in a mine in South Africa. This is the deepest that anyone has ever been.

The biggest cave

The Sarawak Chamber in Malaysia is the biggest cave in the world. It is 700m (2,296ft) long. If you could put football fields down the middle, there would be room for seven.

Things to do

Real fossils take millions of years to form underground. You can make a model of a fossil for yourself.

You will need:

a lump of plasticine

a bag of modelling plaster from a
    model shop

a jug of water

an old bowl and
    spoon

some shells,
bumpy stones or a fossil

Flatten the plasticine a bit, then press a shell into it. Do not press it in too far. Take the shell out very carefully.

Put two handfuls of plaster into the bowl. Add a little water at a time and mix it in. The plaster is ready to use when it drips from the spoon.

Digging for creatures

Use a spade to dig into a patch of garden or waste ground. How many different creatures can you dig up?

Put them in a plastic box. Draw them and try to find out what they are. Afterwards, put them back again.

You could do the same with a stone or a fossil.

Spoon the plaster into the hole in the playdough. Leave it for ten minutes to go hard. Peel away the playdough to find the shell fossil.

Underground quiz

Here are some questions to see how much you can remember from this part of the book. If you get stuck, look back at the pages for help. Check the answers at the bottom of this page.

1. Where was the world's first underground railway built?

2. What is the name for the rocky remains of animals and plants?

3. Most houses are built on top of a very strong base. What is it called?

4. A rabbits' home has lots of burrows. What is it called?

5. What is the pipe called that takes fresh water to your home?

6. The Earth is made up of layers. What is the top layer called?

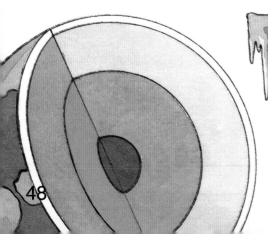

7. What is the name for rocky "icicles" which hang down in a cave?

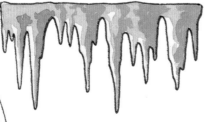

8. What is the name for rocky towers which grow on a cave floor?

Answers: 1.London 2.Fossils 3.The foundation 4.A warren 5.The mains pipe 6.The crust 7.Stalactites 8.Stalagmites

48

WHAT'S UNDER THE SEA?

Consultant: Sheila Anderson

CONTENTS

Under the sea

Under the sea lies an amazing world of strange sea creatures, coral reefs, hidden wrecks and buried pipelines.

Different things go on in different parts of the sea, from the surface down to the seabed.

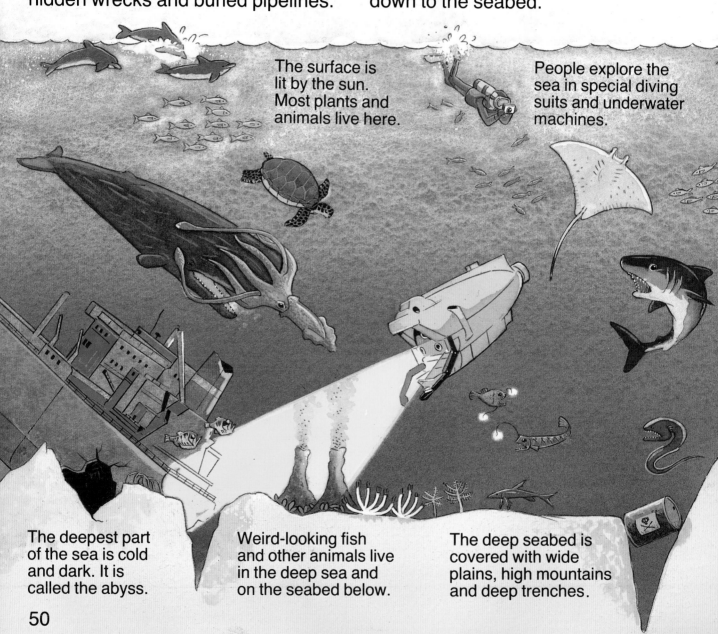

The surface is lit by the sun. Most plants and animals live here.

People explore the sea in special diving suits and underwater machines.

The deepest part of the sea is cold and dark. It is called the abyss.

Weird-looking fish and other animals live in the deep sea and on the seabed below.

The deep seabed is covered with wide plains, high mountains and deep trenches.

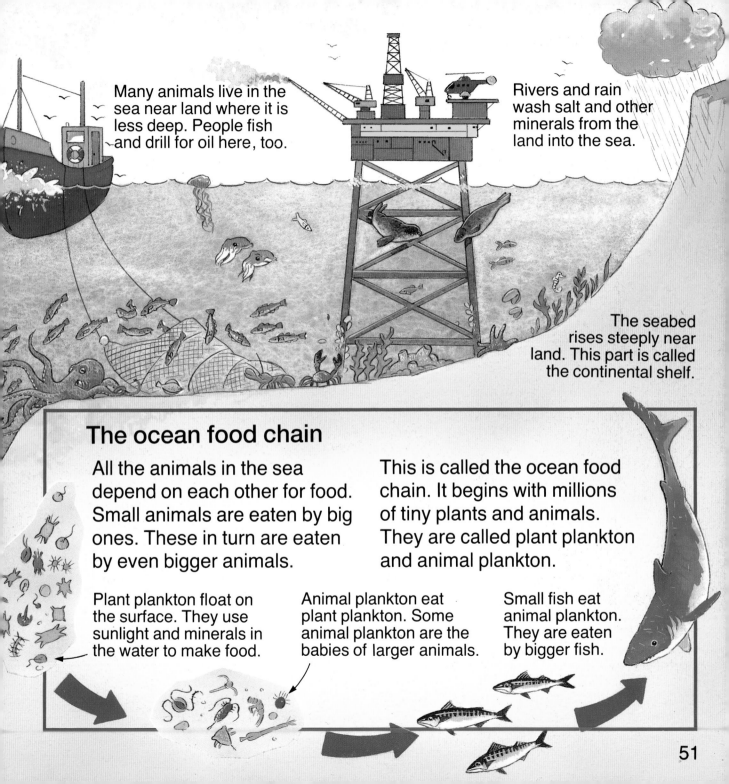

Many animals live in the sea near land where it is less deep. People fish and drill for oil here, too.

Rivers and rain wash salt and other minerals from the land into the sea.

The seabed rises steeply near land. This part is called the continental shelf.

The ocean food chain

All the animals in the sea depend on each other for food. Small animals are eaten by big ones. These in turn are eaten by even bigger animals.

This is called the ocean food chain. It begins with millions of tiny plants and animals. They are called plant plankton and animal plankton.

Plant plankton float on the surface. They use sunlight and minerals in the water to make food.

Animal plankton eat plant plankton. Some animal plankton are the babies of larger animals.

Small fish eat animal plankton. They are eaten by bigger fish.

51

Seas of the world

Over two-thirds of the Earth's surface is covered by sea. Different parts have different names and the largest areas are called oceans. All of the world's seas and oceans are linked together.

The warmest seas lie near the Equator, an imaginary line around the middle of the Earth.

The coldest seas lie near the North and South Poles, far away from the Equator.

Currents

Water moves around the oceans in underwater rivers called currents. Warm currents flow near the surface but cold ones flow deeper down. This is because cold water is heavier than warm water.

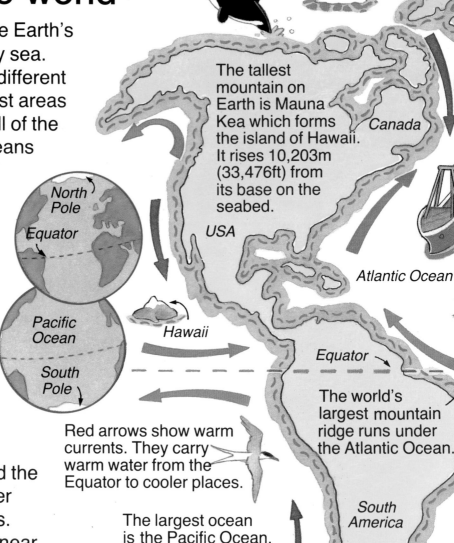

North Pole

Equator

Pacific Ocean

South Pole

The tallest mountain on Earth is Mauna Kea which forms the island of Hawaii. It rises 10,203m (33,476ft) from its base on the seabed.

USA

Canada

Atlantic Ocean

Hawaii

Equator

The world's largest mountain ridge runs under the Atlantic Ocean.

South America

Red arrows show warm currents. They carry warm water from the Equator to cooler places.

The largest ocean is the Pacific Ocean. It covers about one third of the world.

Blue arrows show cold currents. They carry cold water from the Poles to warmer places.

52

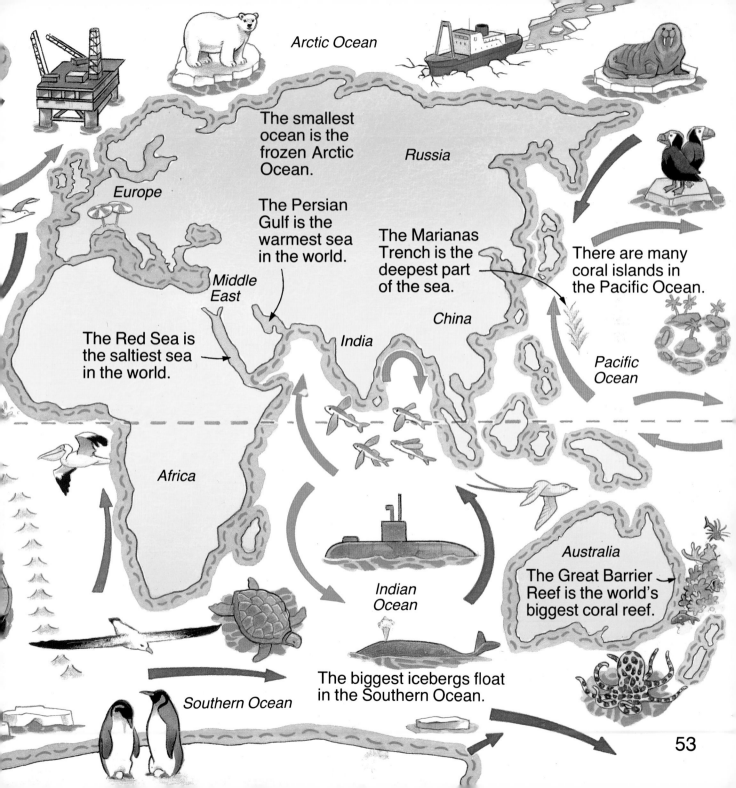

Arctic Ocean

The smallest ocean is the frozen Arctic Ocean.

Russia

Europe

The Persian Gulf is the warmest sea in the world.

The Marianas Trench is the deepest part of the sea.

Middle East

There are many coral islands in the Pacific Ocean.

The Red Sea is the saltiest sea in the world.

India

China

Pacific Ocean

Africa

Indian Ocean

Australia

The Great Barrier Reef is the world's biggest coral reef.

The biggest icebergs float in the Southern Ocean.

Southern Ocean

53

What is a fish?

Over 20,000 kinds of fish live in the sea. Fish are scaly animals with fins. They are also cold-blooded. This means that their bodies are always the same temperature as the sea.

Keeping afloat

Most fish have a bag of air like a small, thin balloon inside them. This is called a swim bladder. It helps them to stay afloat in the water without having to swim.

How do fish breathe?

Fish need oxygen to live. They cannot breathe it through the air, but water also has oxygen in it. Fish have special parts called gills which take oxygen from the water.

Water goes in the mouth, over the gills and out of the gill covers above. Blood in the gills takes in oxygen.

A fish beats its tail from side to side to push itself forward.

Fins help steer and balance the fish.

Slimy scales help fish glide through water.

Lateral line

Gill cover

A sixth sense

Most fish have a line along each side called a lateral line. This helps them to sense the movements that other animals make in the water.

54

Deep-sea fish

Some of the strangest fish live in the deep sea where it is dark and cold. They have special ways of finding food.

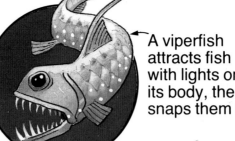

A viperfish attracts fish with lights on its body, then snaps them up.

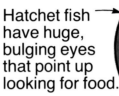

An angler fish has a light on its head. Fish swim up to it and are gobbled up.

Hatchet fish have huge, bulging eyes that point up looking for food.

A gulper eel gulps down fish with its gaping mouth and long, stretchy belly.

Sharks and rays

Sharks and rays are among the biggest fish in the sea. They do not have swim bladders so they must keep swimming or they will sink.

Sharks have rows of razor-sharp teeth. When the front ones wear down, back ones move forward to take their place.

Great white shark

The manta ray flaps its side fins to swim. It leaps out of the water to escape danger.

Whales

Whales are the largest animals in the sea. They are not fish, but mammals. Mammals breathe air. They are also warm-blooded. This means that their bodies stay warm even when the sea is cold.

Baleen whales gulp in water and krill, then sift the water out through their baleen.

Baleen

Baleen whales

Some whales, such as humpback whales, do not have teeth. They have fringes of bristle called baleen instead. These whales eat tiny shrimps called krill.

A whale comes to the surface to breathe air through a blow-hole on its head.

Blow-hole

Krill

Whales have lots of fat, called blubber, to keep them warm.

Whales in danger

So many big whales have been hunted that there are far fewer left. Most countries have stopped hunting them, but a few still do.

Humpback whale

Whales with teeth

Other whales, such as sperm whales, have sharp teeth to eat fish, squid and other animals. They find food by making clicking noises.

These clicks bounce off animals in their way and send back echoes. The whale listens to the echoes to find out where the animal is.

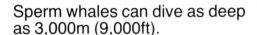

Clicks sent out by the whale.

Echoes bouncing back from the squid.

Sperm whales can dive as deep as 3,000m (9,000ft).

Squid is the sperm whale's main food.

Whale sizes

Whales come in all sizes. The smallest ones are porpoises and dolphins and the biggest ones are blue whales. Blue whales are the largest animals in the world.

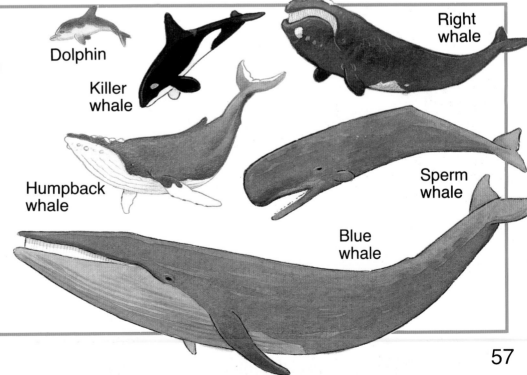

Dolphin

Killer whale

Right whale

Humpback whale

Sperm whale

Blue whale

Coral reefs

Coral reefs are like beautiful underwater gardens. They grow in warm, shallow seas and are home to all sorts of fish and other animals.

What are corals?

Corals come in all shapes and sizes. They are built up from the stony skeletons of tiny animals called coral polyps. Polyps live on the surface of corals. When they die, new polyps grow on top.

This is a close-up of a coral polyp cut in half. It uses its tentacles to sting animal plankton and put them in its mouth.

Tentacle

Mouth

Skeleton

Most coral polyps hide in their cup-shaped skeletons during the day. They come out to feed at night.

Corals build up into giant reefs over thousands of years.

Many fish have bright patterns to help them hide among corals.

A porcupine fish blows itself up into a spiky ball to stop others from eating it.

Parrot fish have strong teeth to crunch up corals.

Sea anemones are like big coral polyps. They feed in the same way.

Clown fish can hide safely among sea anemones without being stung.

Giant clams close their shells when they are in danger.

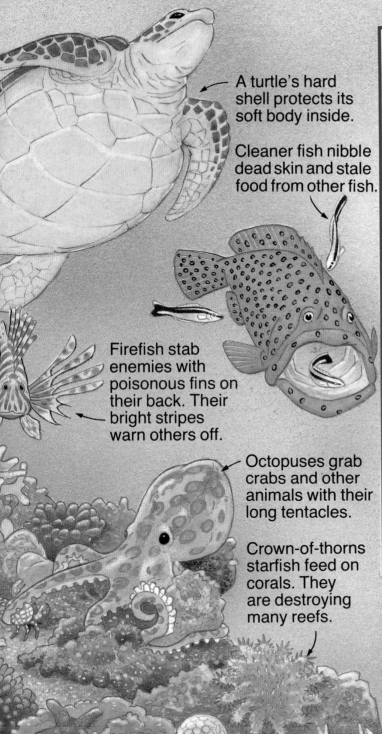

A turtle's hard shell protects its soft body inside.

Cleaner fish nibble dead skin and stale food from other fish.

Firefish stab enemies with poisonous fins on their back. Their bright stripes warn others off.

Octopuses grab crabs and other animals with their long tentacles.

Crown-of-thorns starfish feed on corals. They are destroying many reefs.

Coral islands

Coral islands often start as a fringe of coral which grows around the tip of an undersea volcano.

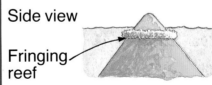

Side view

Fringing reef

The tip of the volcano forms an island.

The seabed slowly sinks taking the volcano down with it. The coral grows up to form a barrier reef.

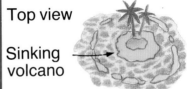

Top view

Sinking volcano

Barrier reefs grow offshore.

The sunken volcano leaves behind a ring of coral islands called an atoll. The sea inside is called a lagoon.

Top view

Lagoon

Coral atolls have no island inside.

Reefs under threat

Many reefs are damaged by people collecting coral and by pollution. A few are now protected as sea parks.

Icy seas

The coldest seas lie near the North and South Poles. They are called polar seas. They freeze over in autumn and melt in spring. Even so, many animals live in and around them.

Chunks of ice called icebergs float in polar seas. Some break off from rivers of ice called glaciers which slide off the land. Others break off from shelves of ice which stick out from the land.

As they melt, icebergs break up into smaller chunks called bergy bits.

Icebergs slowly drift into warmer water where they melt.

Most of an iceberg lies underwater. Only the tip shows above.

Penguins

Penguins are sea birds which cannot fly. They use their wings as flippers to swim underwater. Most penguins live in the southern polar seas.

Penguins can swim fast through the water. They leap out of the water to breathe air.

Penguins have a thick layer of fat, called blubber, and waterproof feathers to keep them warm.

Krill

Swarms of krill live in polar seas. Most polar animals eat krill, including whales which feed in polar seas in summer.

Penguins dive down for fish, krill and squid.

Seals

Seals are mammals which live mostly underwater. They come up to the surface to breathe air. Many seals live in the cold polar seas.

In winter, ringed seals scrape holes in the ice to breathe through.

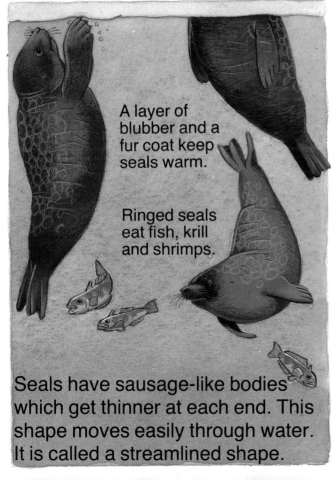

A layer of blubber and a fur coat keep seals warm.

Ringed seals eat fish, krill and shrimps.

Seals have sausage-like bodies which get thinner at each end. This shape moves easily through water. It is called a streamlined shape.

Polar bears

Polar bears live near the North Pole. They are strong swimmers and hunt seals and other animals in the sea and on land.

Polar bears have fur and blubber to keep them warm.

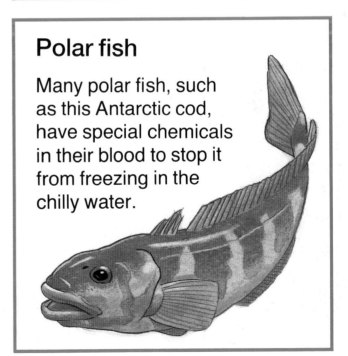

Polar fish

Many polar fish, such as this Antarctic cod, have special chemicals in their blood to stop it from freezing in the chilly water.

61

Divers

Divers do all sorts of work under the sea, from mending pipelines to studying the seabed. Most only go down to 50m (160ft). These divers carry a tank of air on their back to breathe from.

This diving suit keeps water out so the diver stays warm and dry.

Coming up

As divers go down, more water presses on them from above. This is called water pressure. Divers must come up very slowly to get used to changes in pressure.

Deep-sea divers

Deep-sea divers work at about 350m (1,000ft). Most breathe a special mix of gases through a pipe. This is sent down to them from a machine called a diving bell.

One of these pipes carries gas. Another pumps hot water around the suit to keep the diver warm.

Hard suits

Some deep-sea divers wear hard suits which protect them from the pressure of the water. They breathe oxygen from tanks inside.

Part of this suit has been cut away to show the diver inside.

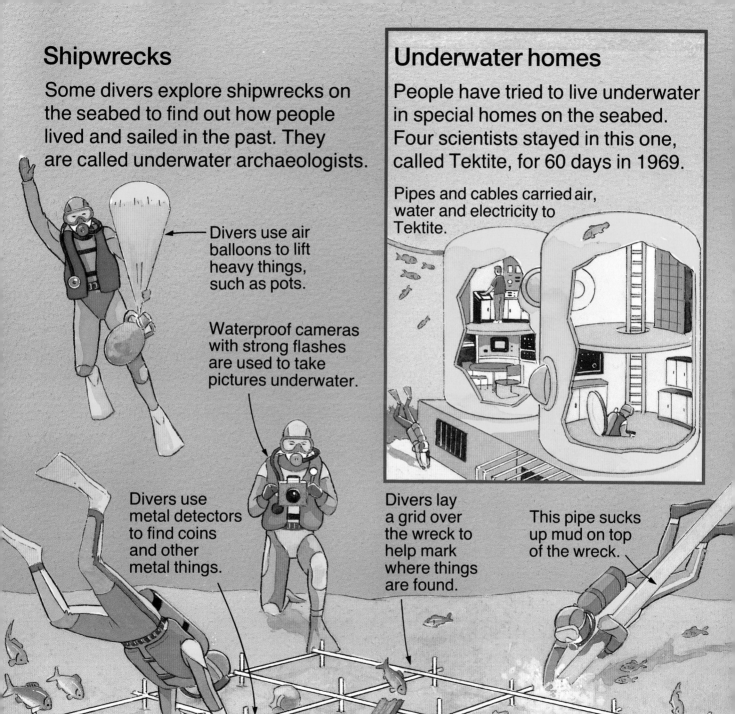

Shipwrecks

Some divers explore shipwrecks on the seabed to find out how people lived and sailed in the past. They are called underwater archaeologists.

Divers use air balloons to lift heavy things, such as pots.

Waterproof cameras with strong flashes are used to take pictures underwater.

Divers use metal detectors to find coins and other metal things.

Underwater homes

People have tried to live underwater in special homes on the seabed. Four scientists stayed in this one, called Tektite, for 60 days in 1969.

Pipes and cables carried air, water and electricity to Tektite.

Divers lay a grid over the wreck to help mark where things are found.

This pipe sucks up mud on top of the wreck.

Underwater machines

Underwater machines called submersibles can go even deeper than divers. They have special tools to work underwater. Some submersibles carry people, but most are undersea robots which are controlled from above.

Going down in submersibles

The French submersible, Nautile, can take people down to 6,000m (19,500ft). Its tools are controlled by the crew inside.

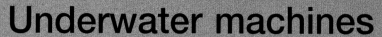

Bright lamps light up the dark water.

These arms can pick up things from the seabed.

Interesting things are stored in this tray to look at later.

Cameras take pictures and films underwater.

Giant batteries power Nautile.

The crew breathe air in the cabin. They look out of windows at the front.

Strong walls protect Nautile from the crushing water pressure outside.

Submarines

Submarines are big underwater ships which are used by navies.

Here you can see how tanks inside a submarine help it go up and down.

The tanks are filled with water to let the submarine go down. The water makes it heavy enough to sink.

The tanks are closed to let the submarine stay at the same depth.

The tanks are filled with air to make the submarine light enough to rise. The air pushes the water out.

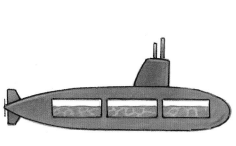

Bathyscaphs

A bathyscaph is a submersible which explores the deepest oceans. It has a cabin below for the crew.

In 1960, the bathyscaph Trieste dived almost 11km (7 miles) to the bottom of the Marianas Trench.

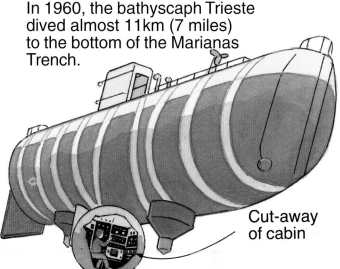

Cut-away of cabin

ROVs

Underwater robots are also known as ROVs. This one is used to mend and bury telephone cables on the seabed.

This ROV blasts a trench in the seabed to bury the cable in.

A line controls the ROV from above.

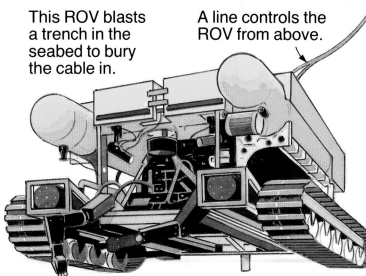

65

The seabed

The Earth's surface is made up of big pieces called plates. These move slowly on a layer of hot rock called the mantle. This picture shows some of the plates which make up the seabed.

Undersea volcanoes are formed by melted rock, called magma, oozing up through the seabed. The magma cools and hardens into layers of rock. It slowly builds up to form volcanoes.

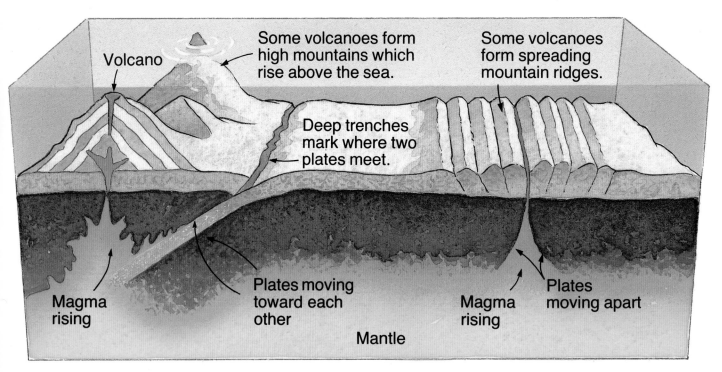

Volcano

Some volcanoes form high mountains which rise above the sea.

Some volcanoes form spreading mountain ridges.

Deep trenches mark where two plates meet.

Magma rising

Plates moving toward each other

Magma rising

Plates moving apart

Mantle

Disappearing seabed

Seabed is always being destroyed. When two plates move toward each other, one plunges underneath. Parts of it melt into magma. Some of this magma may rise to form volcanoes.

New seabed

New seabed is always being made. This happens as two plates move apart. Magma wells up to fill the gap. It forms spreading mountain ridges as it hardens to make new seabed.

Hot springs

Scientists have found hot springs near plate edges. Here, seawater seeps into cracks in the seabed and is heated by hot rocks below. It gushes back up through the seabed in a hot jet.

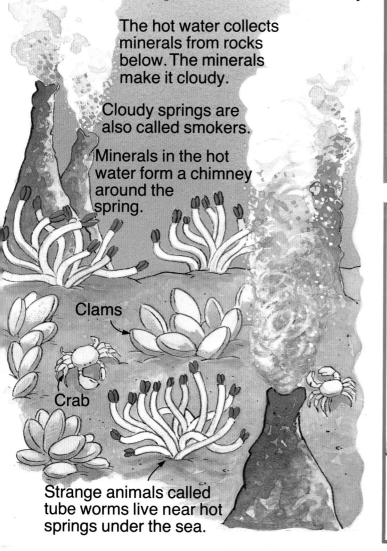

The hot water collects minerals from rocks below. The minerals make it cloudy.

Cloudy springs are also called smokers.

Minerals in the hot water form a chimney around the spring.

Clams

Crab

Strange animals called tube worms live near hot springs under the sea.

How deep is the sea?

People find out how deep the sea is by timing how long sounds take to echo back from the seabed. They put the different depths together to make a map of the seabed.

A machine called an echo sounder sends out sounds and times their echoes as the ship moves along.

Sound waves

Echoes

Tunnels under the sea

Giant drilling machines can bore huge tunnels through the seabed. The longest railway tunnel under the sea is the Channel Tunnel between England and France.

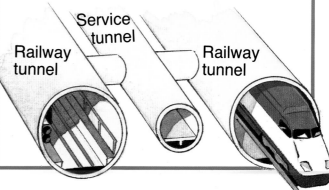

Service tunnel

Railway tunnel

Railway tunnel

Drilling for oil

Giant drilling rigs search for oil far below the seabed. Some rigs stand on the seabed and others float on tanks in the water. They must be strong enough to stand up to rough seas and weather.

This tower is called a derrick. It helps lower the drill pipe into the seabed.

Helicopters carry crew and supplies.

Strong chains and anchors hold the rig down to the seabed below.

ROV

Divers and ROVs check the rig and do repairs underwater.

Diving bell

More pipe is added to the drill as it goes deeper.

These tanks are filled with water to make the rig float lower in the sea.

The drill bit

The tip of the drill is called the bit. It has sharp teeth made of steel or diamonds to cut through rock. When they wear out, the drill is pulled up and the bit is changed.

Drill bit

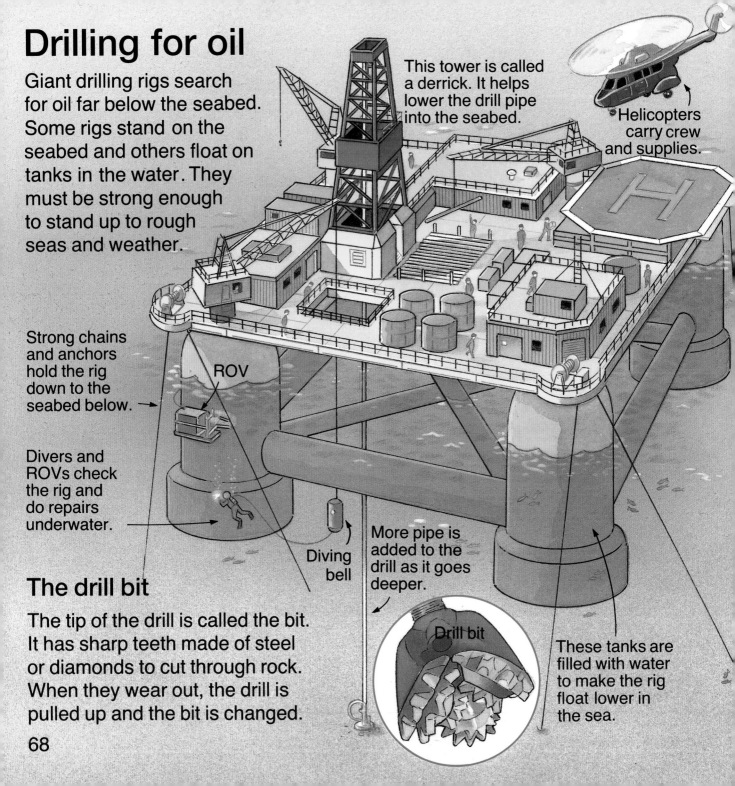

Pumping oil up

Once oil is found, the rig is taken away. A bigger production platform is built to drill more wells and pump oil up.

Several hundred people live and work on a platform.

Gas flare

This platform has a hollow, concrete base to store oil and weigh the platform down.

Gas often comes up with oil. It may be piped to shore or burned off in a flare.

Carrying oil ashore

Pipelines and tankers carry oil to shore where it is used to make fuel, electricity, plastics, paint and glue.

The biggest oil tankers can carry 500,000 tonnes (tons) of oil.

Pipelines are coated with concrete to weigh them down. Some are buried, too.

Layers of rock

Oil wells

Drops of oil and gas are trapped in some rocks like water in a sponge.

Gas

Oil

Oil spills

Oil tankers sometimes leak and spill oil into the sea. Oil spills do a lot of harm and are very difficult and expensive to clean.

Oil spills choke and smother animals which cannot escape.

How oil is formed

Oil is formed over millions of years from tiny, dead sea animals. These were buried by mud which hardened into rock. The rock slowly crushed their rotting remains into oil and gas.

69

Using the seas

For thousands of years, people have fished the seas for food. Today, modern fishing boats can catch huge amounts of fish at a time in giant nets.

Shellfish

All kinds of shellfish come from the sea. People usually fish for them in shallow seas near the shore.

Oysters   Mussels   Cockles
Crab   Lobster   Prawns

Trawl nets scoop up fish on or near the seabed.

Some fish swim in big groups called shoals. Purse nets are pulled around whole shoals.

Drift nets are stretched out to catch fish. Unfortunately they trap other animals, too.

Some nets have bigger holes. These let baby fish slip out.

Overfishing

Too many fish are caught in some parts of the sea. Baby ones are caught before they can grow and breed. Some countries have agreed to catch fewer fish because of this.

Mining minerals

Useful rocks, minerals and precious stones are also taken from the sea.

Sand and gravel are scooped up from the seabed near coasts and used for building.

In some hot countries, seawater is collected in flat pans near shore. It dries up in the sun, leaving salt behind.

Diamonds are sucked up from the seabed off southwest Africa.

Lumps of a valuable metal called manganese lie on the seabed below the Pacific Ocean. They may one day be mined.

Pearls are found in oysters. They grow around grit inside oysters.

Keeping seas clean

People dump waste in the sea from factories, sewage works and nuclear power stations. Too much waste can pollute the water. Countries need to work together to keep seas clean.

Polluted water can poison fish and other animals.

Lost nets and litter can choke and trap animals.

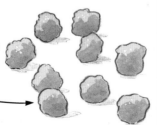

How deep do they dive?

Guess which of these animals, people or machines can dive the deepest. Then follow the ropes and anchors to see if you guessed right.

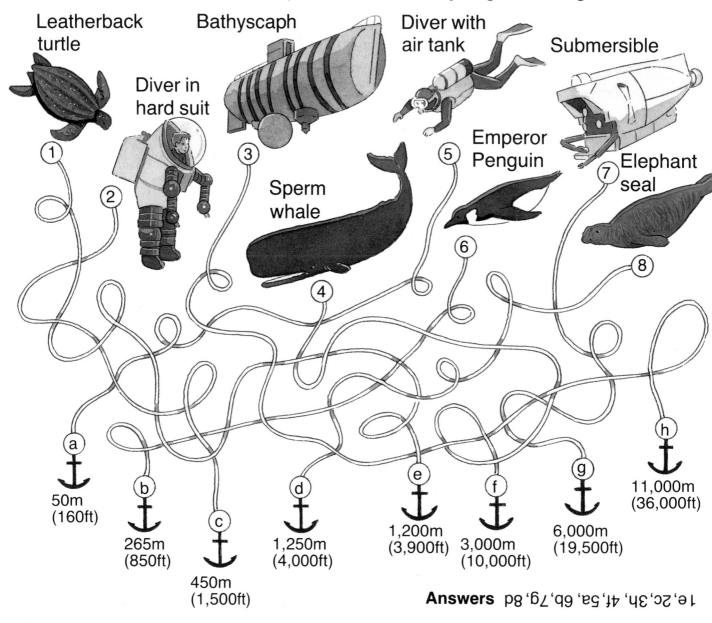

Leatherback turtle

Diver in hard suit

Bathyscaph

Diver with air tank

Submersible

Sperm whale

Emperor Penguin

Elephant seal

1
2
3
4
5
6
7
8

a
50m (160ft)

b
265m (850ft)

c
450m (1,500ft)

d
1,250m (4,000ft)

e
1,200m (3,900ft)

f
3,000m (10,000ft)

g
6,000m (19,500ft)

h
11,000m (36,000ft)

Answers 1e, 2c, 3h, 4f, 5a, 6b, 7g, 8d

WHAT MAKES IT RAIN?

CONTENTS

All about rain

When grey clouds start to fill the sky, this often means that rain is on the way.

The rainwater runs down drains, or into streams, rivers and lakes. Some of it makes puddles on the ground.

Sometimes there is too much rain and sometimes there is not enough. When the air is cold snow may fall.

74

When the rain stops and the sun comes out, puddles on the ground get smaller and smaller.

Where does the water go when it dries up? How does water get into the sky to make more rain?

What is a weather forecast and how is it made? You can find out about these things in this part of the book.

Where the water goes

After a shower of rain, heat from the sun begins to dry up all the water on the ground.

The water turns into tiny droplets in the air, leaving the ground dry. The droplets are so small that you cannot see them. They are called water vapor.

When water dries up, this is called evaporation.

Try this

On a hot day, try this experiment to make water dry up.

Put two plates in a sunny place with a spoonful of water in each one.

Shade one plate with a book.

Look at the plates every hour.

The water in the sun dries up first. Water always evaporates more quickly in the hot sun than it does in the cool shade.

Heating up

If a pan without a lid boils on a high heat for a long time, the water will evaporate and the food burns.

Warm air

When air is warmed, it rises. You cannot see it moving, but you can sometimes see how it takes things up, high into the sky.

Smoke from a fire rises up the chimney and into the sky.

Warm air from a bonfire carries sparks and bits of ash upwards.

Try this

Hold a very thin piece of tissue paper over a hot air heater.

Never let the paper get too close.

The air warmed by the heater rises and lifts the paper.

The sun's heat

Warm air and water vapor.

Air rises when it is warmed by the sun. It carries water vapor from the land and sea up into the sky.

Water in the air

When water vapor in the air cools, it turns into water drops which you can see. This is called condensation.

Your warm, damp breath makes steamy clouds on a cold day.

Steam from hot water is water vapor which has turned into tiny drops in the cold air.

Try this

Breathe hard on a cold mirror and see what happens.

The water vapor in your breath collects on the mirror and makes it mist up.

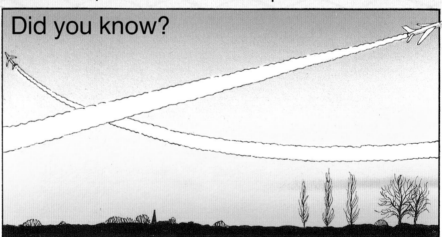

Did you know?

You can sometimes see water vapor very high in the sky behind airplanes.

It is pushed out of the engines and leaves long trails of white cloud in the cold air.

Dew

On a warm day there is a lot of water vapor in the air. This is because warm air can hold more water vapor than cold air.

As the warm air cools down at night, some of its water vapour condenses. It turns into water drops on leaves and cool ground.

These water drops are called dew. You can see it on the ground in the early morning. The sun soon dries it up.

Frost

If the air gets very cold at night, dew freezes into frost.

Sometimes it is so cold that dew does not form. Water vapor condenses straight into frost.

Frost is often so thick and white that it looks like a covering of snow on the ground.

Fog

Fog is lots of tiny water drops in the air. The drops form when air full of water vapor cools near the ground.

Cold air

The heat from the sun bounces off the ground and warms the air near it. The air higher up in the sky is much colder. It is so cold that high mountain tops are snowy all year.

How clouds form

Every day water from the sea evaporates in the sun.

The warm air near the ground carries the water vapor up into the sky.

The cold air makes the water vapor condense into groups of tiny drops or ice crystals. We see them as clouds.

Did you know?

In some parts of the world people can sunbathe on a beach and see snow on the high mountains.

Above the clouds

When you take off in an airplane, you can go through the clouds and fly above them. The sun shines up there all the time during the day.

Inside a cloud

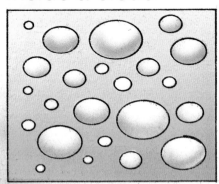

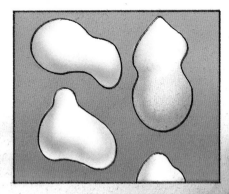

The millions of tiny water droplets which make a rain cloud are different sizes.

Big drops fall and bump into smaller ones. They join and make bigger drops.

When the water drops are heavy enough they fall to Earth as drops of rain.

Below the clouds

The rainwater collects in seas, lakes, rivers and puddles. When it stops raining the sun will start to dry up this water.

Snowy weather

How snowflakes form

Most water drops in high clouds freeze into tiny specks of ice in the cold air.

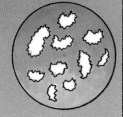

As they fall, more water freezes on them. They become ice crystals.

When the crystals are big enough, they join together and fall as snowflakes.

Falling snowflakes soften in warmer air. They stick together easily. Sticky snow makes good snowballs.

Snowflake facts

All snowflakes are a six-sided shape.

Millions of snowflakes have fallen to Earth, but nobody has ever found two which are exactly the same.

Did you know?

People have seen huge snowflakes the size of large plates.

Avalanches

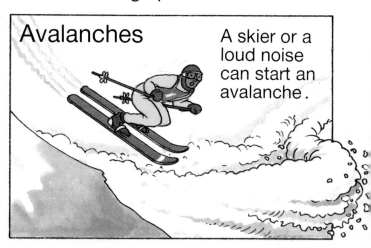

A skier or a loud noise can start an avalanche.

An avalanche is lots of snow which slides down a steep mountain slope. This may happen when the weather gets warmer and snow starts to melt.

Hail

Hailstones are hard lumps of ice which form inside a storm cloud. They fall to the ground very quickly in a hailstorm.

Raindrops freeze into ice pellets at the top of a storm cloud.

Air currents toss them up and down. More water freezes on to them.

When the pellets are too heavy to stay up, they fall as hailstones.

Inside a hailstone

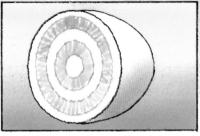

If you cut a hailstone you would see the layers of frozen water.

Did you know?

The biggest hailstone was 19cm (7½in) across, which is nearly as big as a football.

Hailstone damage

Big hailstones can make dents in cars and break windows. A bad hailstorm can flatten a field of corn in just a few minutes.

Rainbows

Next time it rains and the sun is shining at the same time, look for a rainbow.

How a rainbow is made

A ray of light looks white but it is really made up of many colors.

When sun shines through a raindrop the water splits the light into all its colors.

sunlight

raindrop

The colors bounce off the back of the drop and bend as they come out.

A rainbow appears when sunlight shines on falling drops of water in a waterfall.

Rainbow colors

There are seven main colors in a rainbow and they are always in the same order – red, orange, yellow, green, blue, indigo and violet.

Try this

Put a glass of water on a sheet of white paper. Make sure it is in front of a sunny window.

When the sun shines brightly, a small rainbow will appear on the paper.

Thunderstorms

Tall, dark clouds often bring a storm with thunder and flashes of lightning.

What is lightning?

A kind of electricity, called static electricity, starts to build up in a storm cloud.

When there is too much, it jumps from the cloud in a huge, hot spark. This spark is the flash of lightning which you see in the sky.

Why we hear thunder

A flash of lightning heats the air around it very quickly. It starts a huge wave of air which grows bigger and bigger. This makes the thunder which you hear.

Lightning can go from cloud to cloud, or from the cloud down to the ground.

Try this

Make your own spark of static electricity.

Press a large lump of playdough or clay onto a tin tray to make a handle.

Hold the clay and rub the tray round and round on top of a thick plastic bag.

In the dark, hold something metal near the corner of the tray. Watch a spark jump away.

Water on the ground

In a town, rainwater runs down the drains. It is carried away by underground pipes.

In the country, rainwater runs down slopes and into streams, rivers and lakes. Some soaks into the ground.

As a stream flows along, it is joined by more water from springs and from under the ground.

A river finds the easiest way across the land.

The water trickles down through the soil. It goes into underground streams and wells, then it travels on under the ground.

Sometimes underground water comes out of the side of a hill as a spring. Most streams start from a spring in this way.

Snow and ice melt when the weather warms up. The water runs away and soaks into the ground.

As the rivers, streams and springs make their way to the sea, some of their water evaporates.

More streams join together and they form a river.

A small river which flows into a bigger one is called a tributary.

Some water collects in hollows in the ground. This is how lakes are formed.

The river mouth is where the water runs out into the sea and ends its journey.

Water evaporates from the sea every day. The tiny invisible droplets will soon collect to make more clouds.

Too much rain

A flood sometimes happens when there is a very heavy rainstorm, or if it rains for a long time. The water cannot all seep away into the ground and it runs onto the land. Streams and rivers overflow with water.

Snow and ice

Floods sometimes happen in the spring when snow and ice start to melt. The water cannot soak into the soil because the ground is still frozen hard underneath.

Stopping the water

A dam is a wall which is built across a river to make a lake. It holds the water back and can also be used to control floods.

A sudden flood

A flood which happens very suddenly is called a flash flood. It happens when a huge amount of rain falls in one place in a very short time.

There was a flash flood in New South Wales, Australia, in April 1989. The water swept away roads, bridges, cars, buildings and animals.

Living with rain

People in Indonesia build houses on stilts. They will be safe above the water when the floods come.

Moving away

The people of Barotseland, Zambia, move away when the floodwaters come. They take all their belongings to higher ground.

The driest places

Drought

In some places it does not rain for many weeks. There is not enough water to drink or grow plants. This dry time is called a drought.

Did you know?

A strange plant grows in Africa's Namib Desert. Its leaves soak up water vapor from fog and it lives for at least a thousand years.

Deserts are the driest places in the world. In some places it does not rain for years. Any water evaporates quickly in the hot sunshine.

Cacti are desert plants which store the water they need in their stems.

In the United States, water from the Colorado River runs along canals to the Sonoran Desert. It is pumped onto the dry land to grow crops.

Did you know?

A camel can live for as long as ten days in the desert without drinking.

Its body slowly turns fat in the hump into the water it needs.

The long roots of the mesquite plant find water 53m (174ft) under the ground.

Kangaroo rats never drink. Their bodies have a special way of making water from the dry seeds which they eat.

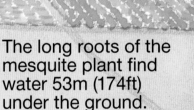

Desert flowers

Seeds of flowers lie in the dry soil waiting for rain. When it falls, the flowers bloom very quickly but they only live for a day or two.

What kind of weather?

A weather forecast tells you what the weather is going to be like. You can see it on television, hear it on the radio or read it in the newspaper.

Weather forecasts can help you decide what to wear or where to go for the day.

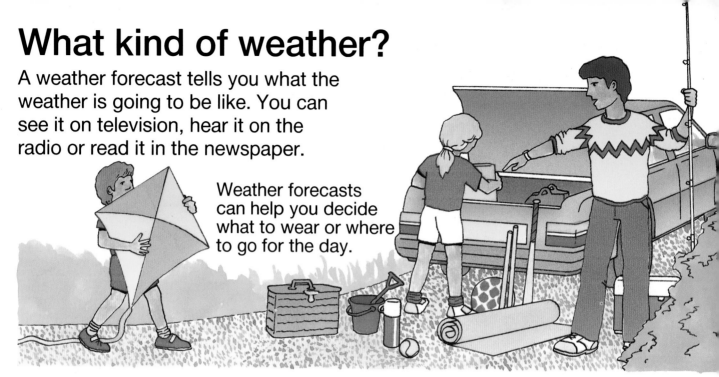

People who need to know

An aircraft pilot needs to know what the weather will be like on the flight.

A fisherman needs to know if the weather at sea is going to be fine or stormy.

A farmer uses weather forecasts every day. He needs good weather for a lot of his work.

Making a weather forecast

A weather station is where facts about the weather are collected at certain times every day.

More facts come from satellites which study the weather from space.

They measure the wind speed and the water vapor in the air. They even measure the temperature.

Forecasters collect facts from weather stations around the world and from satellites. They use the facts to make weather charts.

They use these charts to help make a weather forecast. This tells you what the weather will be like over the next few days.

Useful words

You can find these words in this part of the book. The pictures will help you remember what the words mean.

canal
This is a special waterway built for ships and to carry water across land.

condensation
This is tiny drops of water you see on cold things. It forms when warm, damp air touches something cold.

dam
This is a wall built to hold water back and make a lake.

desert
This is a dry place, where it hardly ever rains. Only a few plants grow.

dew
This is the name for the small drops of water which form on cool ground, leaves and plants.

evaporate
This is what happens when water dries up. It turns into tiny, invisible water drops in the air.

flood
This is when lots of water covers the land, after too much rain.

frost
This is tiny drops of frozen water which appear on the ground and on other things in cold weather.

hail
This is the name for lumps of ice which form in a storm cloud.

fog
This is tiny drops of water which you can see in the air. It looks like patches of low cloud.

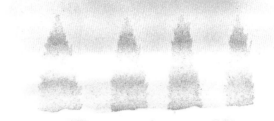

water vapor
This is the name for tiny droplets of water in the air. The droplets are so small you cannot see them.

weather satellite
This is a machine sent into space to study the weather around the Earth.

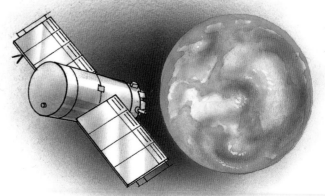

95

Making a weather chart

Trace this chart on to a piece of paper. Go outside every morning and afternoon to see what the weather is like, then choose the right weather sign to put in the box. There may be two kinds of weather.

	morning	afternoon
Monday		
Tuesday		
Wednesday		
Thursday		
Friday		
Saturday		
Sunday		

sun

cloud

rain

snow

wind

hail

thunder and lightning

Does the weather change much? Has it been sunny or cloudy? Has there been rain or snow?

You could make up some new weather signs yourself. Can you think of one for frost or fog?

WHY IS NIGHT DARK?

Science consultant: Sue Becklake

CONTENTS

In this part of the book you can find out why night is dark. There is lots more to know about nighttime. Here are some things you may have noticed. They are all explained later on.

Have you ever noticed that the Moon can be different shapes?

On a clear night you can see lots of stars. Do you know what happens to them during the day?

Sometimes the Moon and stars are hidden by clouds or fog. They are still there, even though you cannot see them.

Town lights

Electric lights in towns or cities can also make it seem less dark at night.

If you live in a town or city, you may have noticed how the sky glows at night.

All the lights you see here run on electricity. Have you wondered how electric light bulbs work?

Do you know how people lit up the dark before electric lights were invented?

When it is day where you are, it is night on the other side of the world.

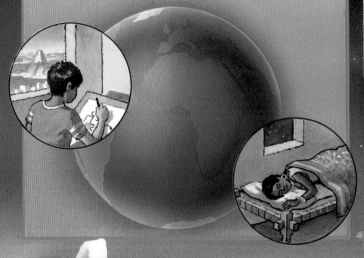

As you go to bed some animals are just waking up. They sleep in the day and look for food at night.

Do you know how these animals find their way in the dark?

The Sun never sets here in summer. It is called the midnight Sun.

Some places do not get dark at night in summer, or get light during the day in winter.

People used to think everything in space moved around the Earth. They invented reasons to explain night and dark. The next pages explain what really happens.

Light and dark

It would always be dark on Earth if the Sun did not rise every morning. The Sun gives us light each day.

The Sun is a giant ball of incredibly hot, glowing gases. It gives out a huge amount of light and heat. Without it nothing could live or grow on Earth.

The Sun always shines, even when clouds keep you from seeing it.

A chariot of fire

The Sun is so important to life on Earth that hundreds of years ago people worshiped it as a god.

The Ancient Greeks believed that their Sun god Helios drove his chariot across the sky in the day. He rested his horses at night.

The Sun in the sky

On sunny days you can see the Sun rise, move across the sky and set.*

People used to think this was because the Sun moved around the Earth.

In the morning the Sun rises in one part of the sky.

At midday you can see the Sun high above you.

In the evening the Sun sets in another part of the sky.

The spinning Earth

Now people know that the Sun does not move around the Earth.

It is really the Earth that spins around and around in space.

The Sun only shines on one half of the spinning Earth.

The half facing the Sun is in the light. It is daytime there.

The sunlight cannot reach the other half of the Earth.

The half facing away from the Sun is in the dark. It is night there.

Sunrise and sunset

As your part of the Earth turns towards the Sun it begins to get light. This is when the Sun seems to rise.

As your part of the Earth turns away from the Sun, it begins to get dark. This is when the Sun seems to set.

See for yourself

You need a flashlight and a ball. Mark a spot on the ball for your home with tape or a pen. Make your room dark.

Ask someone to turn the ball while you shine the flashlight on it. See how the spot goes in and out of the light.

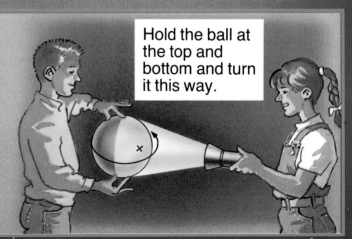

Hold the ball at the top and bottom and turn it this way.

101

Day turns to night

The Earth makes one full spin every 24 hours. During this time most places have a day and a night. But not all places have day and night at the same time. As one place spins into the light, another spins out of it.

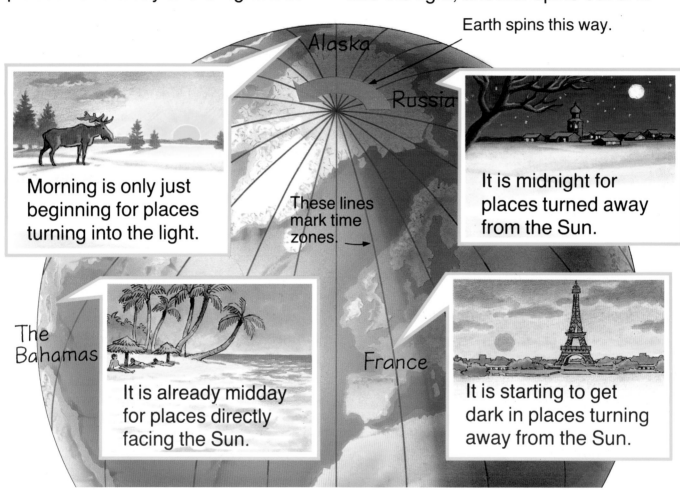

Earth spins this way.

Alaska

Russia

These lines mark time zones.

Morning is only just beginning for places turning into the light.

It is midnight for places turned away from the Sun.

The Bahamas

France

It is already midday for places directly facing the Sun.

It is starting to get dark in places turning away from the Sun.

Sometimes we need to know what time it is in another country. To help us people have divided the world into 24 "slices" called time zones.

You can see them in this picture. Each place in one zone has the same time. But it is one hour earlier or later in the zones on either side.

How time zones work

Some very big countries, such as the United States of America, go across many time zones. This country is made up of smaller parts called states. The time lines on this map bend to keep some whole states in one zone.

This way is West. Each zone is an hour earlier going this way.

This way is East. Each zone is an hour later going this way.

1 o'clock   2 o'clock   3 o'clock   4 o'clock

These lines show the time zones.

Saving daylight

In many places the Sun rises early in summer when most people are asleep. This seems a waste of daylight. So lots of places put their clocks forward one hour in summer.

Now the clocks say it is time to get up one hour earlier than in winter.

The clocks go back again one hour in winter.

Changing the time

When you travel into a new zone you change the time on your watch. You put it forward one hour for each zone you cross going East, and back one hour for each zone going West.

There is one special line called the International date-line. When you cross it, you change the day of the week, as well as the time.

The seasons

As well as spinning around once each day, the Earth also moves around the Sun. It takes a year to go around once.

The leaning world

The Earth is not quite upright as it spins in space. It leans to one side.

North is this way.

The North Pole is at the top of the Earth.

The top half is called the Northern Hemisphere.

This imaginary line around the middle is called the Equator.

The bottom half is called the Southern Hemisphere.

South is this way.

The South Pole is at the bottom.

The way the Earth leans makes the seasons change in both hemispheres during the year.

The Sun's rays

The Sun's rays shine more directly on the half leaning towards the Sun. Direct rays feel hot. It is summer here.

direct ray

The Sun always shines almost directly on the Equator. It is always hot here.

direct ray

The Sun's rays slant across the half leaning away from the Sun. Slanting rays feel cooler than direct rays because their heat spreads over more ground. It is winter here.

slanting ray

A journey around the Sun

This picture shows the Earth moving around the Sun. The Earth always leans the same way so the Sun shines more directly on the Northern half and then on the Southern half. This gives each half summer and winter. When it is summer in one half, it is winter in the other.

Summer nights

The hemisphere that leans towards the Sun spends more time in sunlight each day. Nights are short.

March

spring

autumn

The poles do not spin out of the sunlight in summer, or into it in winter.

The Equator does not lean towards or away from the Sun. Days and nights are always about equal.

December

winter

summer

June

summer

winter

Spring and autumn

In the middle of spring and autumn neither half leans more towards the Sun. Days and nights are the same length.

September

autumn

Winter nights

The hemisphere that leans away from the Sun does not get many hours of light. Nights are long.

spring

The Moon

Some nights are less dark than others. On a clear night you can usually see the Moon shining brightly.

The Moon looks big and bright in the night sky. But unlike the Sun it does not make its own light.

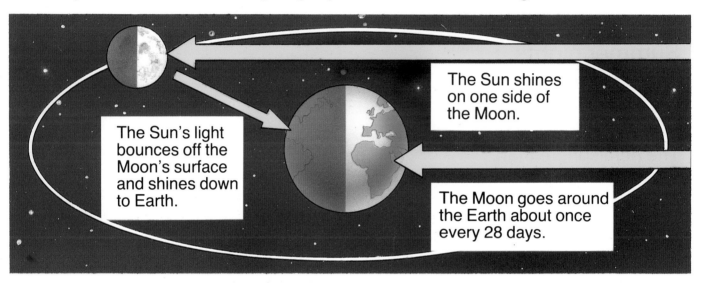

The Sun shines on one side of the Moon.

The Sun's light bounces off the Moon's surface and shines down to Earth.

The Moon goes around the Earth about once every 28 days.

The changing Moon

As the Moon moves you see different amounts of its light side. You could record the shapes on paper.

Draw the shape you see inside a circle. Do it each evening you see the Moon for 28 days. See how it changes.

You cannot really see a New Moon. The Sun lights up the other side.

This is a Crescent Moon. You can see a little of the Moon's light side.

This is a Full Moon. You see all its light side. After this you see less.

Exploring the Moon

The Moon is nearer to Earth than the Sun or stars. It is the first place that people have visited in space.

12 astronauts went to the Moon between 1969 and 1972. Some took a Moon buggy to drive.

Astronauts wear spacesuits on the Moon to protect them from heat and cold and supply them with the air they need.

crater

Footprints will not blow or wash away as there is no wind or rain on the Moon.

There is no air, water or life on the Moon. It is a still and silent place, covered with craters made when space rocks crashed there.

The Man in the Moon

The dark patches you can see on the Moon are flat plains. Some people think they look like a face and call it the Man in the Moon. See if you can see it next time there is a Full Moon.

The Moon's pull

The Earth and Moon both pull things and people down towards them. This pull is called gravity. It makes things feel heavy when you lift them.

The Moon's pull is weaker than the Earth's. This makes things and people feel lighter there.

Astronauts' spacesuits and backpacks are not so heavy on the Moon. Astronauts walk with great bouncy steps.

107

On clear nights you can see hundreds of stars. Each one is a giant ball of hot, glowing gases like the Sun.

The stars look tiny because they are very far away.

The Sun is really a star too. It looks so big because it is our nearest star. Others are bigger but further away.

You cannot see the other stars during the day because the Sun is so bright.

A star is born

Stars are born in a gas and dust cloud. The cloud squeezes into a ball. It gets very hot and glows as a new star.

After millions of years a star swells up and cools. It is now called a red giant. Later, its outer layers drift into space.

Some of the biggest stars explode at the end of their lives. They leave behind new clouds of gas and dust.

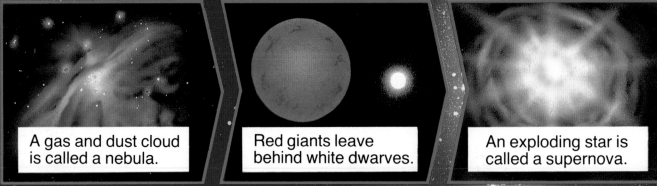

A gas and dust cloud is called a nebula.

Red giants leave behind white dwarves.

An exploding star is called a supernova.

The Milky Way

Stars belong to huge groups called galaxies. The stars you see belong to a galaxy called the Milky Way.

The Earth is also in the Milky Way.

The Milky Way is a spiral shape. It spins slowly through space.

The Sun is one of thousands of millions of stars in the Milky Way.

The Milky Way is one of thousands of millions of galaxies in space.

Star patterns

Long ago people saw patterns in the stars. These patterns are called constellations. You can see different ones from different parts of Earth.

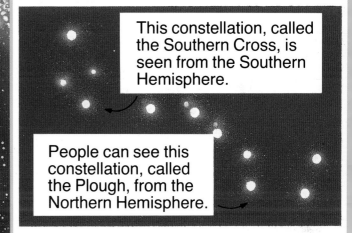

This constellation, called the Southern Cross, is seen from the Southern Hemisphere.

People can see this constellation, called the Plough, from the Northern Hemisphere.

Ask a grown-up to help you find the group seen from your part of Earth.

Sailing by the stars

The stars have always helped sailors find their way. The last two stars in the Plough point to the North Star for example. It shows which way is North.

The Solar System

Our part of the Milky Way is called the Solar System. The Sun is at the center with nine planets and lots of moons and bits of rock going around it. You can see them in this picture.

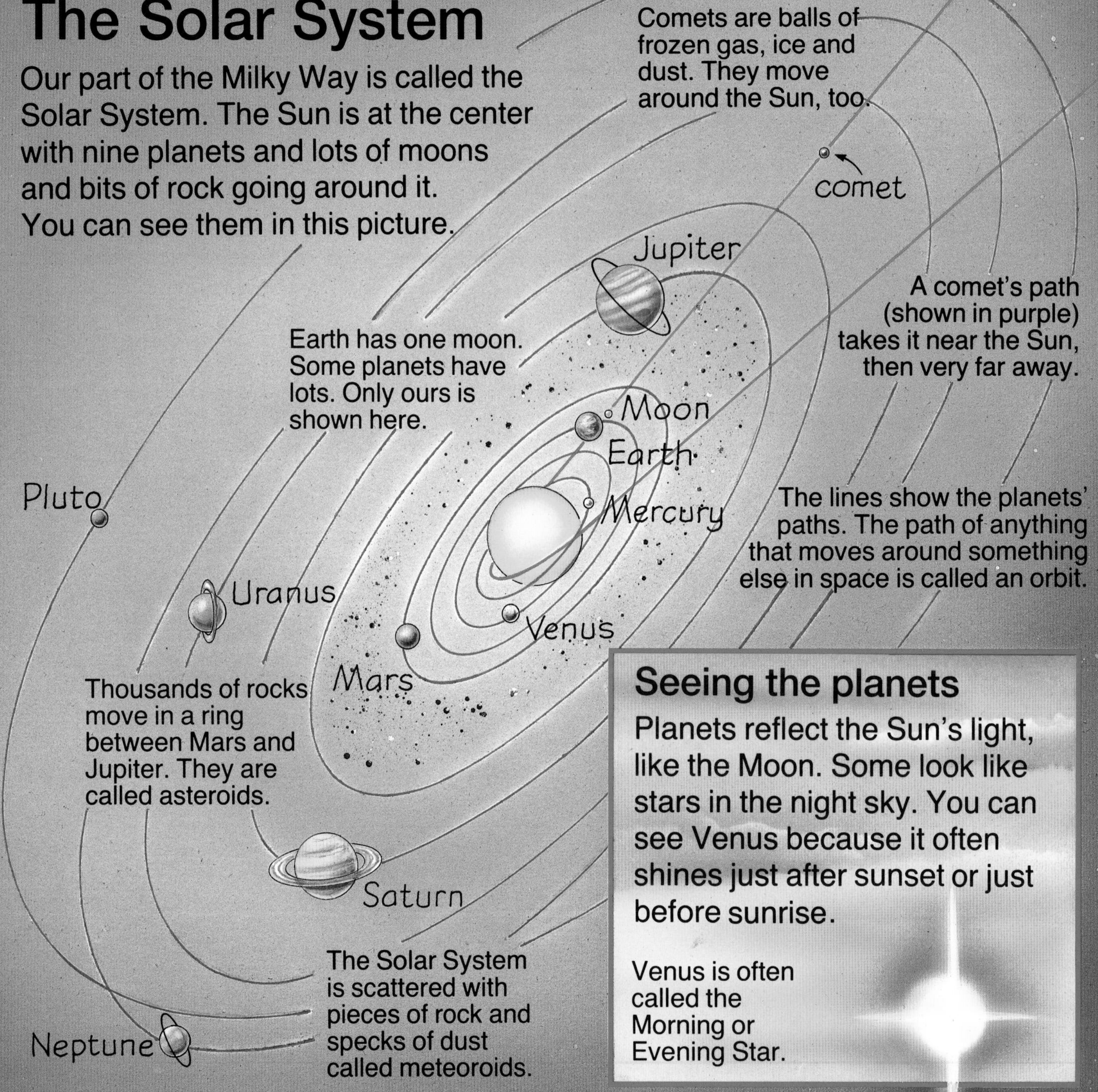

Comets are balls of frozen gas, ice and dust. They move around the Sun, too.

comet

A comet's path (shown in purple) takes it near the Sun, then very far away.

Jupiter

Earth has one moon. Some planets have lots. Only ours is shown here.

Moon
Earth
Mercury

The lines show the planets' paths. The path of anything that moves around something else in space is called an orbit.

Pluto

Uranus

Venus

Thousands of rocks move in a ring between Mars and Jupiter. They are called asteroids.

Mars

Seeing the planets

Planets reflect the Sun's light, like the Moon. Some look like stars in the night sky. You can see Venus because it often shines just after sunset or just before sunrise.

Venus is often called the Morning or Evening Star.

Saturn

The Solar System is scattered with pieces of rock and specks of dust called meteoroids.

Neptune

Night sights

Here are some other bright things you may see in the night sky. Some are natural and others are man-made.

As a comet gets near the Sun, the gas and dust flow into a long, bright tail. You may occasionally see one at night.

Sometimes meteoroids fall into the Earth's air. They burn up, making a bright streak called a meteor or shooting star.

A satellite is a spacecraft. It may send telephone calls, television pictures and other information around the world.

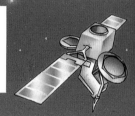

Satellites reflect sunlight and glint like slow-moving stars.

Glowing lights

This colored light is called an aurora.

It begins at about 100km (60 miles) above the ground.

Sometimes the Sun gives out extra bursts of energy. These can make the sky near the Poles glow with slowly changing colors.

Airplanes use lights so they can be seen clearly in the dark.

Town lights reflect off clouds. This can make the sky glow.

People light fireworks at night since they show up best in the dark.

Night life

Some animals come out at night. Most can see well in the dark, and have a good sense of hearing, smell or touch, too. These senses warn them of danger and help them to find food and mates in the dark.

Here you can see some animals that come out when it starts to get dark. These animals are called nocturnal, which means "of the night".

Most bats cannot see well. Some have a special kind of hearing to help them catch moths at night.

Badgers sniff the air for danger before leaving their burrows. The damp night air carries smells well.

Rabbits and deer go further afield at night. The dark helps to hide them from enemies.

Cats and foxes use their long whiskers to feel their way through small gaps.

Owls and cats have big eyes that open up in the dark to let in as much light as possible.

Hedgehogs use their snouts to smell and forage for grubs.

Noises at night

The dark hides friends as well as enemies. Some animals find mates by calling to them.

Frogs croak to let other frogs know where they are.

A male cricket makes a chirping call to a female by rubbing its wings together.

Bat squeaks

Bat squeaks make echoes as they bounce off things such as trees and moths. Bats listen to the echoes to find out where things are.

Bats do not bump into things. They zig-zag to avoid trees, or to catch insects.

Most bat noises are too high for people to hear.

Night glowers

Some insects have a special way of making light in their own bodies.

Glow-worms shine in the dark to attract mates.

Fire-flies flash lights to each other.

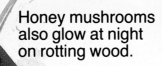

Honey mushrooms also glow at night on rotting wood.

Flowers of the night

Some flowers are also nocturnal. They smell sweeter at night.

The scent attracts moths that get food from the flowers.

Moths also take dust called pollen from one flower to another. This helps new flowers grow.

night-flowering catchfly ➝

How light works

During the day, the Sun's light lets you see shapes and colors.

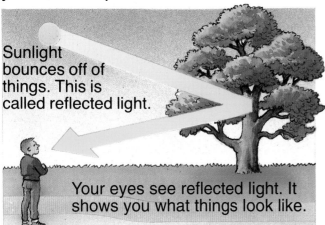

Sunlight bounces off of things. This is called reflected light.

Your eyes see reflected light. It shows you what things look like.

At night there is not enough light to see things clearly.

People travelling at night use lights to see and be seen.

Light and color

Sunlight looks clear but is really made up of many colors. You can see them when the Sun shines through raindrops and makes a rainbow.

Light bends as it goes into a drop of water. Each color bends a different amount. This separates them.

The colors bounce off the back of the drop.

The drop reflects the colors. They bend on their way out.

A green leaf only reflects the green color in sunlight. It takes in, or absorbs, the rest.

This is why it looks green.

Light gives all things their color. When light hits things, some colors are reflected. The rest are taken in. You only see the reflected colors.

Make a color mixer

You can see how many colors make white. Cut out a cardboard circle about 4in wide. Lightly crayon in the rainbow colors.

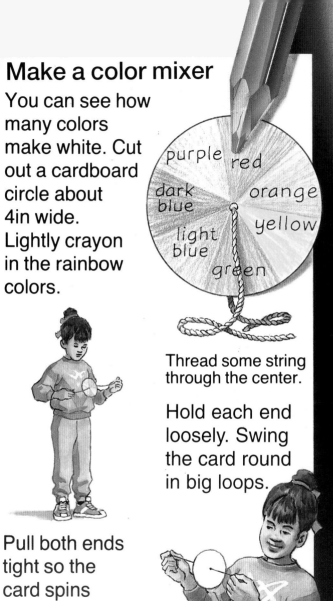

purple
red
dark blue
orange
light blue
yellow
green

Thread some string through the center.

Hold each end loosely. Swing the card round in big loops.

Pull both ends tight so the card spins fast. Look at the colors as the card spins.

The colors blend. If you spin the card very fast, it looks almost white.

Why is sky blue?

In the day the sky is often blue. This is because there is a layer of air around the Earth.

This air is full of dust and drops of water. These scatter the blue color in sunlight more than the other colors.

There is no air in space to scatter the Sun's light. This is why space is black.

A black sky
The sky above the Moon is black even during the day because there is no layer of air around it.

Shadows

Light only moves in straight lines. It leaves dark shadows behind things that stand in its way. That is why the Earth is always dark on one side. The Sun's light cannot bend around it.

Draw your shadow

On a sunny day, you keep some sunlight from reaching the ground. This makes your shadow.

Ask a friend to draw around your shadow on a sunny morning.

Mark where you stood. Do it again at other times of the day.

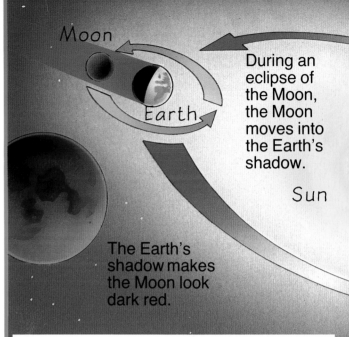

During an eclipse of the Moon, the Moon moves into the Earth's shadow.

The Earth's shadow makes the Moon look dark red.

The Earth's shadow

At times, the Earth is directly between the Sun and Moon. The Sun's rays cannot bend around to light the Moon. This is an eclipse of the Moon.

midday

Shadows always point away from the Sun.

evening

See how your shadow moves and how long it gets, as the Sun moves across the sky.

Day shadows

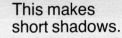

The Sun's rays reach the ground in a short, more direct path.

This makes short shadows.

Shadows are short at midday when the Sun is high in the sky.

During an eclipse of the Sun, all three line up like this.

The sky grows dark for a few minutes and the stars appear.

Moon

Earth

The Moon's shadow

Less often, the Moon moves directly between the Earth and Sun. It blocks out the Sun and casts a shadow on Earth. This is an eclipse of the Sun.

The Sun's rays travel in a longer, slanting path to reach the ground.

Shadows are long and thin.

Shadows are long in the morning and in the evening, when the Sun is low.

Make a shadow clock

Fix a pencil upright on a piece of cardboard with modeling plastic. Put it in a sunny place in the morning.

Draw around the cardboard with chalk to mark its place.

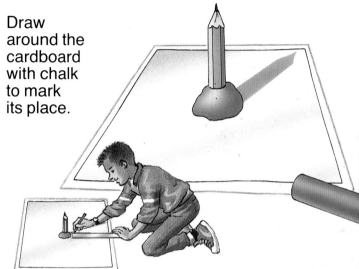

Draw the pencil's shadow. Write the time by the shadow. Do this again every hour.

This clock will only be right for a few weeks. The shadows change as the Sun rises earlier or later during the year.

Put the cardboard in the same position the next day. The shadow will show you roughly what time it is.

117

Lights in the dark

People have always looked for ways to light up the dark, so they could keep on seeing and doing things after the Sun set.

Firelight

The flames blazed with light but also sent out smoke and sparks.

Some early people lit fires by striking two special stones together to make sparks. The sparks set dry leaves on fire.

Oil lamps

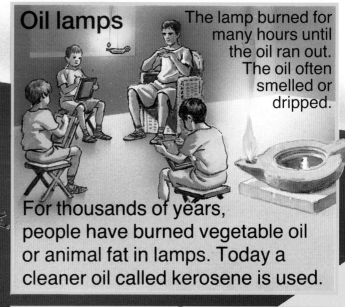

The lamp burned for many hours until the oil ran out. The oil often smelled or dripped.

For thousands of years, people have burned vegetable oil or animal fat in lamps. Today a cleaner oil called kerosene is used.

Candlelight

The weak, flickering flame often smoked or went out. It only lit up a small area.

Candles were made from animal fat or beeswax for thousands of years, too. Now they are also made from paraffin wax.

Gaslight

A glass shade spread the light more evenly.

150 years ago gas was carried to homes and streetlamps through pipes. Gas burned in bright jets of flame when it was lit.

Electric lights

People have only used electric light bulbs for about 100 years. The first one was made by Thomas Edison in 1879. Here you see what happens when you turn on a light or flashlight.

This metal coil is called a filament.

A flashlight makes a strong, steady beam.

A battery inside the flashlight sends electricity to light the bulb. When the electricity is used up, you can put in a new battery.

Electric bulbs are much stronger and brighter than any light used before.

Electricity goes along hidden wires to the light bulb. It makes a metal coil inside the bulb glow white hot.

Guiding lights

At night, lighthouses warn ships of rocks with a strong, flashing light.

"Cat's-eyes" are bits of glass set in rubber blocks.

"Cat's-eyes" in roads reflect car lights back to the driver.

Bright lights on the runway help airplanes land in the dark.

119

Old beliefs

Long ago, people did not always know why it got dark, where the Sun went at night or what the stars were. They made up stories to explain these and other mysterious things such as the Moon's shapes, eclipses and comets.

A basket of darkness

Some Africans said it never got dark until God told the bat to take a basket of darkness to the Moon. The darkness escaped. Since then the bat tries to get it back each night.

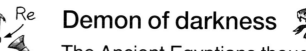

Demon of darkness

The Ancient Egyptians thought their Sun god Re sailed down to the underworld each night and fought a demon snake of darkness. Re always won and sailed up into the sky each day.

A thousand eyes

According to people in India the stars were the eyes of Varuna, their sky god, who saw everything.

Hairy stars

Comets were once thought to be hairy stars. People thought awful things would happen when they saw one.

Eating the Moon

The Ancient Egyptians said the Moon got thin each month because it was attacked and eaten by a black pig. Then it was born again.

Swallowing the Sun

In China, people thought an eclipse of the Sun was a terrible dragon eating the Sun. They beat drums and gongs to scare it away.

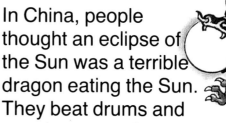

WHAT'S OUT IN SPACE?

Science consultant: Sue Becklake

CONTENTS

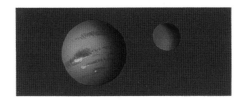

Space watching

At night, when the sky is clear, you can see hundreds of stars far out in space. On most nights you can see the Moon as well.

If you want a better look at the Moon you can use binoculars to make it look bigger and closer.

The Solar System

The things you can see in the sky at night only make up a little of what's out in space. Our planet Earth is in one tiny part of space called the Solar System.

The Solar System is made up of nine planets, lots of moons and lumps of rock called asteroids. There are also balls of ice and rock called comets. Everything moves around the Sun.

Sun

Moons move around planets. Earth has one moon, but some planets have lots.

Jupiter

Mercury

Earth

Moon

Venus

Mars

Astronomers

An astronomer is someone who looks at things in space. People have been doing this for thousands of years.

A modern astronomer uses a telescope to see things further away than you could ever imagine.

This picture shows the order of the planets from the Sun outwards. They are many millions of miles apart. Some are rock, like the Earth. Others are made of liquids and gases.

The Sun is the biggest thing in the Solar System. It is made of glowing, hot gases. But there is much more in space than all of this. Everything we know about is called the Universe.

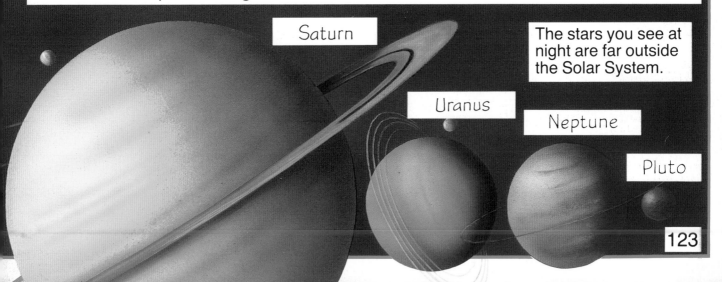

Saturn

The stars you see at night are far outside the Solar System.

Uranus

Neptune

Pluto

Light and dark

The Sun is the only thing in the Solar System which makes light. Nothing else has light of its own.

Astronomers can only see planets and moons because the Sun shines on them and makes them show up.

Moving around

Each planet goes around the Sun on its own invisible path called an orbit.

Earth

Pluto →

Earth takes just over 365 days to orbit the Sun once. This time makes one Earth year.

Planets further away from the Sun than us take much longer to make one orbit. Pluto takes 248 Earth years.

Day and night

As the Earth moves on its long journey around the Sun, it turns all the time. It makes one turn every 24 hours.

When your side of Earth faces the Sun, you have day. When you are turned away from the Sun, it is night.

You cannot always see the Sun, but it shines in space all the time.

Watching the Moon

At night the Moon seems to shine brightly, but the light you see is really from the Sun.

It shines on to half of the Moon all the time and lights it up.

Use binoculars to take a closer look at the Moon. The big dark patches are mainly flat areas called seas, but there is not really any water.

The dark rings are craters. They were made by space rocks which crashed into the Moon.

The Moon's shape

The Moon moves around the Earth all the time. Each night you can see a different amount of the bright side.

Sometimes you can see more of it and sometimes you can see less. The Moon's shape does not really change.

You cannot see a New Moon. The Sun is shining on the other side.

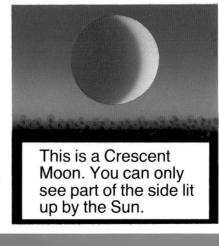

This is a Crescent Moon. You can only see part of the side lit up by the Sun.

This is a Full Moon. You can see all of the bright side.

Going to the Moon

The hardest part of going into space is getting off the ground. This is because of something invisible called gravity. Gravity pulls everything near the Earth back to the ground.

If you throw a ball up in the air it comes down again. It is gravity which pulls the ball back. Without gravity, the ball would go up into space.

Breaking away

A spacecraft going to the Moon has to break away from Earth's gravity. A powerful rocket blasts it into space to escape the strong pull. The spacecraft gets to the Moon in about three days.

space-craft

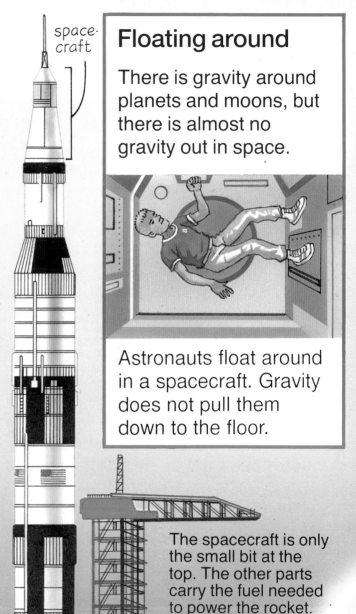

Floating around

There is gravity around planets and moons, but there is almost no gravity out in space.

Astronauts float around in a spacecraft. Gravity does not pull them down to the floor.

The spacecraft is only the small bit at the top. The other parts carry the fuel needed to power the rocket.

launch pad

126

The first moonwalk

The Moon is the only thing in space that people have visited. On July 20, 1969, American astronauts became the first people to land there. They went in the Apollo 11 spacecraft.

When the astronauts walked on the Moon, they seemed to float with each step. This happened because the Moon's gravity is weaker than Earth's, so it did not pull them down so strongly.

Neil Armstrong was the first person to walk on the Moon.

The astronauts left scientific instruments on the Moon. They also collected rock and dust to take back to Earth.

The Lunar Module took the astronauts down to the Moon. Apollo 11 stayed in space.

It was very hot in the sunlight but very cold at night. The astronauts had to take their own air supply in tanks because there is no air on the Moon.

The Moon's surface is dry and dusty. There is no wind to blow the soil about or rain to wash it away. Footprints will stay there forever.

About the Sun

The Sun is the most important thing in the Solar System. It gives the planets their light and heat. Its gravity stops the planets from flying off into space.

The Sun is really a medium-sized star. Many stars you see at night are bigger and brighter than our Sun. They look small because they are so far away.

Where the Sun came from

Scientists think that the Sun and the planets may have formed inside a huge cloud of gas and dust in space.

The gas and dust were squashed together in the middle of the cloud and this part became very hot. This is where the Sun began. The planets formed at about the same time.

What the Sun is like

The Sun is not a ball of rock like the Earth. It is made of hot glowing gases which make it look like a fiery ball. Huge amounts of light and heat come from the surface.

Giant bursts of gas are thrown up from the Sun's surface. They are called flares and prominences. They look like flames.

DANGER

Never look at the Sun with binoculars or a telescope. The strong light will damage your eyes or make you blind.

Hiding the Sun

Sometimes the Moon comes between the Sun and the Earth and covers the Sun up. This is an eclipse of the Sun.

This glow is called the corona. It only shows during an eclipse.

The Moon is much smaller than the Sun but it can hide the Sun from our view. This happens because the Moon is much closer to us.

How it works

You can blot out a ceiling light by holding a coin in front of your eye. Cover the other eye with your hand.

Because the coin is close to your eye it can easily blot out the light which is further away. The Moon can blot out the Sun in the same way.

Sunspots are darker patches. They are cooler than the rest of the surface.

Life on Earth

Nothing would live or grow on Earth without the Sun's light and heat. The Earth's atmosphere only lets through the light and heat we need to live, keeping out the Sun's harmful rays.

129

Exploring the planets

Scientists can find out more about the planets by sending machines called probes out into space. These do not carry people, only special equipment.

Next to the Sun

Mercury is the nearest planet to the Sun. It has mountains and craters like our Moon, but it is much hotter.

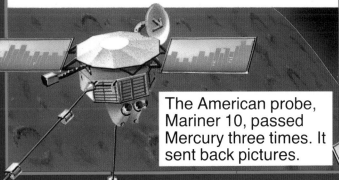

The American probe, Mariner 10, passed Mercury three times. It sent back pictures.

Our nearest planet

Venus is Earth's nearest planet. Its rocky surface is very hot and its air is thick and poisonous.

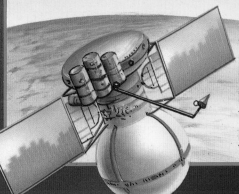

This Russian probe, Venera 9, sent back the first pictures from the surface.

The red planet

This is the American probe, Viking 2.

Mars is the planet which is most like Earth. It has mountains, valleys and volcanoes, but it has a pink sky. Mars is covered with red dust.

Going farther

It takes a probe many years to reach planets far away from the Sun.

The American probe, Voyager 2, has traveled to the edge of the Solar System, exploring planets on the way.

The giants

Jupiter and Saturn are the biggest planets in the Solar System. They are made of gases and liquids. Voyager 2 went to take a look at them.

Saturn has many thin rings made up of small bits of ice. They form bright bands.

Jupiter is the largest of all the planets. It has a patch called the Great Red Spot. This is a huge long-lasting storm.

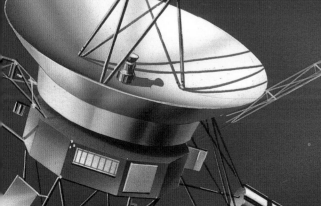

The green planet

Uranus is a gas planet like Jupiter and Saturn. It is the only planet which spins on its side.

Voyager's last visit

The probe, Voyager 2, was sent into space in 1977. It had to travel for 12 years before it reached the planet Neptune.

The smallest planet

Pluto is the smallest planet in the Solar System. It is dark and icy. Its moon, Charon, is about half as big.

Voyager 2 did not visit Pluto, so there is still a lot to find out.

Neptune has a large, dark spot. This may be a storm, like Jupiter's Great Red Spot. There is a smaller spot as well.

Neptune's biggest moon, Triton, is cold and icy. It is a reddish-pink color.

Voyager found six new moons and three faint rings. The rings can only be seen with special instruments.

Scientists call this cloud the scooter because it speeds around Neptune faster than the other clouds.

Voyager 2 left Neptune and traveled out of the Solar System. It will keep going out into space, even when all its machines stop working.

Visitors from space

Comets are balls of ice and rock which move in huge orbits around the Sun. A comet sometimes comes into our part of the Solar System from beyond Pluto.

Halley's Comet comes back every 76 years.

The hard icy middle of the comet is called the nucleus. When the comet gets near the Sun, the ice boils away and makes a tail of gas and dust.

Asteroids

Between Mars and Jupiter there are thousands of rocks called asteroids. They orbit the Sun in a ring called the asteroid belt. Some asteroids are hundreds of miles across.

Meteors

Sometimes a space rock or a speck of space dust speeds into the Earth's air. It burns up making a streak of light called a meteor or a shooting star. You can sometimes see one at night.

Making craters

Big space rocks which crash into planets or moons are called meteorites. Most of our Moon's craters were made by meteorites billions of years ago.

This crater is in the state of Arizona

There used to be craters on Earth, but most of them have been worn away over thousands of years. The crater in this picture is over half a mile across.

Looking at stars

If you could count all the stars you see in the night sky, there would be over a thousand. Astronomers can see millions more with telescopes.

What a star is

A star is a ball of glowing gases just like the Sun, our nearest star. Light from nearly all stars takes thousands of years to reach us on Earth.

Most stars move around each other in groups of two or more. From Earth these groups usually look like a single star. Our Sun is unusual because it is on its own.

Why stars twinkle

Starlight has to pass through the Earth's air before it reaches us. The air moves and changes all the time. It makes a star's light look brighter, then dimmer, so it seems to twinkle.

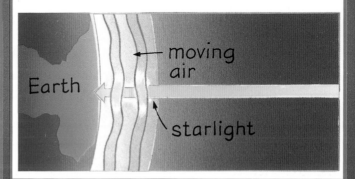

moving air

Earth

starlight

Galaxies

Stars belong to spinning groups called galaxies. There are millions of galaxies and each one has millions of stars. Our Solar System is in a spiral shaped galaxy called the Milky Way.

The life of a star

A star begins in a gas cloud called a nebula. The cloud collapses and squashes together. Its middle gets so hot that it glows as a new star.

The star shines brightly for many millions of years, then it swells up and becomes much cooler. This huge star is called a red giant.

The outer layers of the red giant disappear into space. A piece called the core is left behind. It shrinks to a small star called a white dwarf.

Exploding stars

Some big, heavy stars grow into enormous supergiant stars which can explode into space. An exploding star is called a supernova.

Black holes

When some stars explode they leave a big core. It shrinks and becomes small but very heavy. Its strong gravity sucks everything in, even light. This is called a black hole.

Space shuttles

The Americans and the Russians have both built new kinds of spacecraft called space shuttles. The American shuttle first flew in 1981.

It blasts into space like a rocket, but it comes back to land on a runway like a glider. It can travel into space again and again.

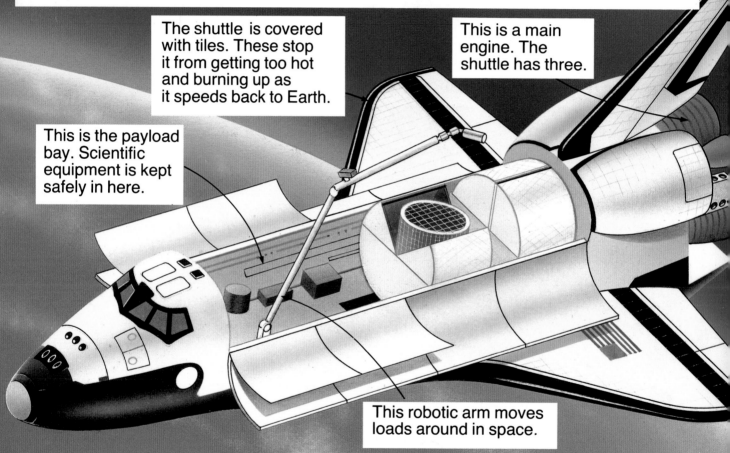

The shuttle is covered with tiles. These stop it from getting too hot and burning up as it speeds back to Earth.

This is a main engine. The shuttle has three.

This is the payload bay. Scientific equipment is kept safely in here.

This robotic arm moves loads around in space.

Inside the American shuttle there is room for seven astronauts. They can launch machines called satellites into space from the payload bay.

On some flights, a special room called Spacelab is put inside the payload bay. Scientists do all kinds of experiments in here.

The flying armchair

Sometimes an astronaut leaves the shuttle to work out in space. He is strapped into a machine which is often called the "flying armchair".

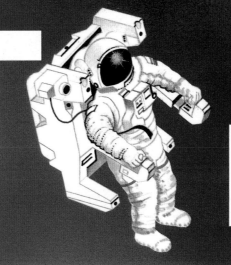

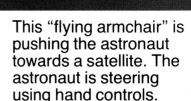

This "flying armchair" is pushing the astronaut towards a satellite. The astronaut is steering using hand controls.

Space journey

The shuttle is blasted into space by its own engines and two large booster rockets.

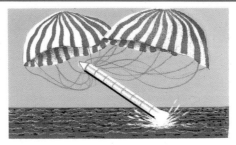

The rockets parachute into the sea when their fuel is used up. They will be used again.

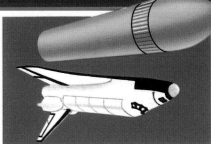

When the shuttle has used all the fuel in the huge tank, the tank falls away.

In orbit, the payload bay doors open. The astronauts begin to work and do experiments.

When the shuttle comes back to Earth it gets red hot because it is going so fast.

The shuttle does not use engines to land. It glides down onto the long runway.

137

A satellite is a thing which moves around something bigger than itself in space. There are natural satellites such as moons. They orbit planets.

The satellites on these pages are machines. They are launched into orbit by rocket or Space Shuttle. They carry equipment to do their work.

High above the world

Different kinds of satellites are put into different orbits. Some move in high orbits, around the middle of the Earth. They move in time with Earth so they stay above the same place.

This satellite beams television pictures and telephone calls around the world.

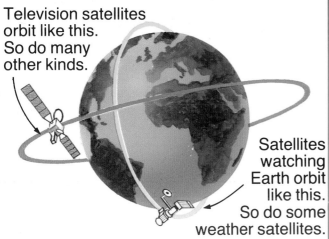

Television satellites orbit like this. So do many other kinds.

Satellites watching Earth orbit like this. So do some weather satellites.

Other satellites make low orbits over the top of the Earth. They go around it several times a day. The Earth turns below them, so they pass over a different part on each orbit.

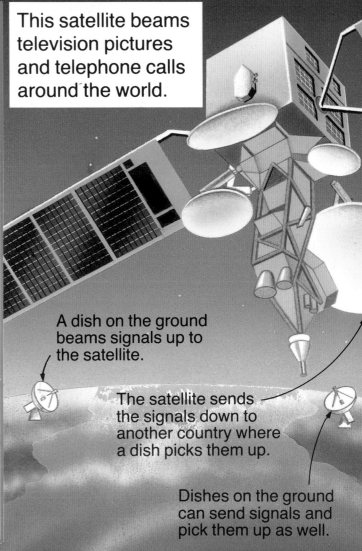

A dish on the ground beams signals up to the satellite.

The satellite sends the signals down to another country where a dish picks them up.

Dishes on the ground can send signals and pick them up as well.

The small squares on the panels are solar cells. They change sunlight into electricity to power the satellite.

There are hundreds of satellites orbiting Earth. In the night sky they look like slowly moving stars.

Some houses have their own small satellite dishes to pick up television signals.

Watching the weather

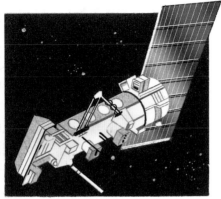

This satellite takes pictures of clouds moving around the Earth and measures the temperature of the air.

The information is beamed down to Earth. Scientists use it to work out what the weather may be like.

Watching space

This astronomy satellite looks out into space. It can see things that scientists cannot see from Earth.

The satellite information can help scientists find out about things such as black holes or galaxies.

Space stations

A space station is a kind of satellite. It is big enough for people to live and work inside. Astronauts travel to the station once it is in orbit.

The first space stations

America and Russia have both launched space stations. The Russians sent up their first Salyut station in 1971. The Americans launched Skylab in 1973.

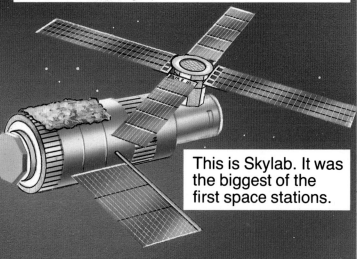

This is Skylab. It was the biggest of the first space stations.

The space stations were launched on top of rockets. Astronauts visited them for a few weeks at a time and sometimes worked outside in space.

Living in space

Astronauts have to learn new ways of doing ordinary things like washing and eating. These are more difficult to do in space as everything floats around.

This special shower is like a bag. It stops water drops from floating about.

Most space food is dried. Astronauts have to add water before they eat it.

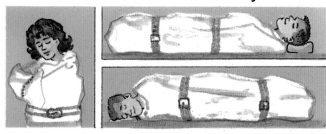

Astronauts can sleep any way up in space. They don't float about because they are strapped into sleeping bags.

Staying in Mir

The first Salyut stations only stayed in orbit for a few months. Now people have lived in space for over a year.

In 1986 the Russians launched a new space station called Mir. Extra parts called modules have been added.

This spacecraft is called Progress. It brings food and fuel from Earth.

This is the Kvant module. It is used specially for watching things out in space.

This is a docking bay. The Soyuz spacecraft is about to join on here.

The Americans are planning a new space station called Freedom. It will be built in space a piece at a time and put together by astronauts. The parts will be taken up by shuttle.

Scientists in Mir do experiments. They also make things which are hard to make on Earth because of gravity's pull.

The future in space

Scientists have made many amazing discoveries in space. Now they are making new plans and inventing new machines to help them learn more.

Telescope in space

The Hubble Space Telescope orbits high above Earth. It sees much further into space than astronomers can from the ground. It may discover far off planets with signs of life on them.

More about probes

New probes will orbit the giant planets, Jupiter and Saturn. One called Galileo is going to Jupiter. Another, called Cassini, is going to Saturn.

Galileo can send a smaller probe down into Jupiter's clouds.

The probes can also visit some of the moons circling the planets. They can send pictures and information back to Earth over several years.

Space planes

There may soon be an airplane which can fly into space and then speed to anywhere on Earth in an hour.

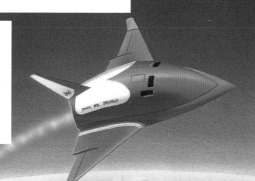

Space planes would also be able to carry satellites out into space and visit space stations.

Building on the Moon

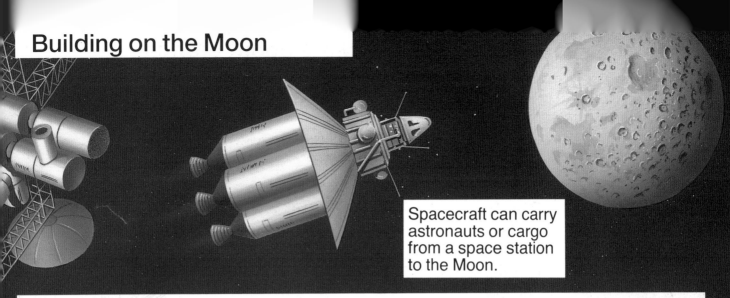

Spacecraft can carry astronauts or cargo from a space station to the Moon.

Astronauts may soon go back to the Moon. They would build a Moon Base for people to live in.

Some of the astronauts at the base may study space. Others may try to find new ways of building on the Moon.

Going to Mars

Mars is the next place astronauts will visit in the Solar System because it is most like Earth and quite near. There are already plans to send people there.

It would take at least six months to travel to Mars. But one day there may be a base there, like the one planned for the Moon.

Space quiz

Here are nine questions about space. The answers are in this part of the book. Can you remember them? Write them down on a piece of paper.

What do astronomers use to help them see far into space?

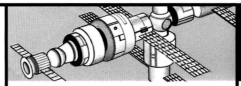

Which country launched a space station called Mir in 1986?

What is the name of Neptune's biggest, icy-cold moon?

Which gas planet spins on its side, almost lying down?

Which spacecraft took people to the Moon for the first time?

Which machines beam television signals around the world from space?

Which was the last planet that Voyager 2 visited?

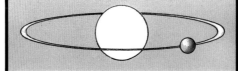

What is the name for a planet's path around the Sun?

What is the name for the rocks which form a belt in space?

Now write down the first letter of each answer. Put the letters in the right order to make a word which means space traveler.

Answers

Telescope, Russia, Triton, Uranus, Apollo 11, satellites, Neptune, orbit, asteroids. When you put the first letters of the words in the right order they spell astronaut.

Index

First published in 1995 by Usborne Publishing Ltd, 83-85 Saffron Hill, London EC1N 8RT, England. Copyright © Usborne Publishing Ltd, 1995. The name Usborne and the device 🎈 are Trade Marks of Usborne Publishing Ltd. All rights reserved. No part of this publication may be reproduced, stored in a retrieval stystem or transmitted in any form or by any means, electronic, mechanical, photocopying, recording or otherwise, without the prior permission of the publisher. Printed in Italy.